T0182542

# THE MORTAL AND IMMORTAL LIFE OF THE GIRL FROM MILAN

Domenico Starnone

# THE MORTAL AND IMMORTAL LIFE OF THE GIRL FROM MILAN

*Translated from the Italian
by Oonagh Stransky*

Europa
*editions*

Europa Editions
27 Union Square West, Suite 302
New York NY 10003
www.europaeditions.com
info@europaeditions.com

Translation by Oonagh Stransky
Original title: *Vita mortale e immortale della bambina di Milano*
Translation copyright © 2024 by Europa Editions

Library of Congress Cataloging in Publication Data is available
ISBN 979-8-88966-047-7

Starnone, Domenico
The Mortal and Immortal Life of the Girl from Milan

Cover illustration by Marina Marcolin

Cover design by Ginevra Rapisardi

Prepress by Grafica Punto Print – Rome

Printed in Canada

For Alberto Cozzella,
Pierangelo Guerriero,
Giovanni Polara:
classmates and friends,
in alphabetical order

# THE MORTAL AND
# IMMORTAL LIFE
# OF THE GIRL
# FROM MILAN

## 1.

Between the ages of eight and nine, I set out to find the pit of the dead. At school, in Italian class, I had recently learned about the legend of Orpheus and how he travelled to the underworld to bring back his girlfriend, Eurydice, who, unhappily, had wound up there after getting bitten by a snake. My plan was to do the same for a girl who was not my girlfriend but who might be if I managed to lead her back above ground from below, charming cockroaches, skunks, mice, and shrews along the way. The trick was to never turn around to look at her, which was harder for me than for Orpheus, with whom I believed I had a fair amount in common. I, too, was a poet, but in secret; I composed deeply tragic poems if I didn't catch sight of the girl at least once a day, which was rare because she lived across the street from me in a brand new, sky-blue building.

It all started one Sunday in March. The windows of our fourth-floor apartment looked out onto the girl's large third-floor balcony and its stone parapet. I was an unhappy child by nature, the girl was the opposite. The sun never shone in our house, it always seemed to shine at the girl's. Her balcony was filled with colorful flowers, my windowsill was bare, at the very most a grey rag hung from a metal wire after my grandmother used it to mop the floor. That

Sunday I started to notice the balcony, the flowers, and the happiness of the girl, who had pitch black hair like Lilyth, the Indian wife of Tex Willer, a cowboy comic that my uncle and I both liked to read.

It looked like she was pretending to be a wind-up ballerina, hopping here and there with her arms above her head and every so often doing a pirouette. From inside came her mother's voice, now and then calling out genteel reminders, like, be careful, don't get sweaty, or, I don't know, easy does it with the pirouettes or you'll bump into the glass door and get hurt. The girl always replied delicately, don't worry, *mammina*, I'm being careful. Mother and daughter spoke to each other like people in books or on the radio, making me yearn less for the words themselves, which I've since forgotten, but for their enchanting sound, which was so different from anything I had heard at home, where we only spoke dialect.

I spent entire mornings at the window, dying to cast off my actual self, transform into a handsome, clean, new person, capable of uttering sweet poetic words straight out of my primer, settle on her balcony, within those sounds and colors, and live forever by her side, asking her every so often and very politely: may I please touch your braids?

At one point, however, she noticed me, and I stepped back in embarrassment. I don't think she liked that. She stopped dancing, stared directly at my window, and started dancing even more energetically. And because I carefully remained out of sight, she decided to do something that took my breath away. With not a little effort, she climbed onto the stone parapet, stood up, and started dancing like a ballerina up and down the narrow ledge.

How beautiful her little body was against the sunlit

windows, her arms above her head, twirling boldly, so exposed to death. I stepped forward so that she could see me, ready to throw myself into the abyss with her if she were to fall.

## 2.

Seeing how one year before, Mr. Benagosti, my elementary school teacher, had told my mother that I was destined for great things, it seemed that finding the entrance to the pit of the dead, raising the lid that covered it, and descending into its depths would be an easy enough task to accomplish. Much of the information I had gathered about the dangerous cavern came from my maternal grandmother, who knew a lot about the hereafter thanks to friends, acquaintances, and relatives who had recently been killed by bombs or in battles either on sea or land—or from frequent conversations with her husband, whose life had been cut short two years after they were married.

What I liked about my grandmother was that I never felt shy around her, mainly because she loved me more than her own children—my mother and uncle—but also because she held no authority within our home. We treated her like a wordless servant, whose only task was to obey our orders and work. As a result, I'd ask her endless questions about whatever subject crossed my mind. I must've been very persistent because sometimes she called me *petrusinognemenèst*, meaning that I was like parsley in soup, chopped parsley, I was everywhere, like the flies that flew around the steamy kitchen in the summer, their wings sometimes growing heavy with moisture, making them fall into the soup pot. Go away, she'd say, what do you want from me? Buzz off, shoo, shoo, shoo. She'd try and brush me off, but then she'd laugh, and I'd start to laugh, too, and occasionally I'd even tickle her so hard she'd say, stop, stop, you're going to make me wet my pants, scoot, go away. But of course, I never did. I was practically mute back then, always on my own, somber, both at home and school. I only opened up to her, and she was as mute with others as I was. She kept her words deep inside, using them only with me, if at all.

She first started telling me the story about the pit of the dead the year before, around Christmas. I was feeling sad and had asked her: how does a person die? While swiftly plucking a recently slaughtered chicken with a look of revulsion on her face, she answered me absent-mindedly: you lie down on the ground and stop breathing forever. Forever? I asked. Forever, she replied. But then she got worried—maybe because she saw me lie down on the freezing cold floor, and while it might not have killed me, it could've easily led to catarrhal bronchitis—and she called me over—*vienaccàbelloranònna*—to where she was standing with the dead chicken half-submerged in boiling water. What's the matter? What's going on? Who hurt you? No one. So why do you want to die? I told her I didn't want to die, I just wanted to spend a little time dead and then get back up. She explained that you can't be dead just for a little, unless you're Jesus, who came back to life after three days. The best thing I could do, she suggested, would be to stay alive forever, and not get distracted and end up dead by mistake. Then, to get across just how awful it was down there, she started to tell me about the pit of the dead.

The entrance, she began, has a cover. This cover—I can still remember each and every word she said—is made of marble and has a lock, a chain, and a bolt, because if people don't close it like they're supposed to, all the skeletons down there that still have a little flesh on them will try to sneak out, together with the rats that scurry in and out of those dirty yellow sheets they wrap around people when they die. Once you raise the cover, you have to pull it shut behind you right away, then go down some steps, but they don't lead to a hallway or sitting room with lots of furniture or some ballroom with crystal chandeliers and gents and ladies and damsels, no, but into a stormy cloud of dirt with thunderbolts and lightning and rain that comes down in buckets and stinks like rotting flesh, and a wind—what a wind, Mimí!—so strong it grinds down mountains and fills the air with powdery dust, yellow like tuff. In addition to the moaning wind and the thunder from the endless storms, she went on to say, there's the constant sound of hammering and chiseling from all the dead people in their tattered shrouds, all men, watched over by boy-angels and girl-angels with red eyes and purple robes, long hair fluttering in the wind, and wings like this chicken, but black like a crow's, either pulled in tight behind them or spread out wide, depending on what they have to do. The dead men toil at crushing enormous blocks of hard marble and granite into pebbles, boulders that extend all the way out to sea, where huge waves of mud crash over them, spraying rotten foam, just like when you squeeze a rotten orange and worms come out. *Ahmaronnamía*, so many dead men. And dead women, too, and always in distress. Because everything around them quakes and trembles in that terrible wind—the mountains, the sky with its dirt clouds and the foul sewage-water that rains down sideways across the stormy sea—there's always something cracking open in the distance, sometimes the whole landscape splits apart, and the clouds come crashing down like tidal waves. And when that happens, the dead women, all wrapped up tight in their shrouds, have to run over there and sew it back up either with needles and thread, or with relatively modern looking sewing machines, patching up the mountains and sky and sea with strips of suede, while the angels, their eyes growing even redder with rage, scream at them: what are you doing? What the hell are you thinking? You idiots, you whores, get back to work, just do your work.

My mind reeled at her stories of those constantly whipping winds and earthquakes and tidal waves, and I listened with my mouth open wide. Later, though, I realized that her story contained quite a few contradictions. My grandmother's accounts didn't exactly shine with precision, and I always had to tighten them up a bit. She had left school in second grade, I was already in third and, therefore, I was clearly smarter. When I forced her to go back and clarify a few things, sometimes all she gave me was half a sentence, other times she told me longer and more detailed stories. Then I'd reconfigure all the details inside my head, welding one to the other with my imagination.

Even so, I was still full of doubts. Where was this marble cover? Was it in the courtyard of our building or beyond the main entrance, and if so, was it to the left, or right? You had to lift it up—fine, I got that—and go down a bunch of stairs, and then surprise, surprise, you walked into a wide-open space with clouds, rain, wind, thunder, and flashes of lightning, but was there electricity down there? A light switch? And if you needed something, who could you ask?

When I pestered my grandmother for details, it was as though she'd forgotten what she'd already told me, and I had to remind her of everything. Once, when filling in the gaps, she went into great detail about the black-feathered angels, who, according to her, were mobsters and spent all their time flapping around in the dust, insulting the hard-working men and women who were busy hammering and sewing. People who work, Mimí, are never bad—she taught me—it's the people who don't work, who get fat off the labors of others who are pieces of shit, and there are so many of them out there! People who think they come straight from Abraham's nuts, who just want to boss people around: do this, do that, do it now. Her husband, my grandfather—who died when he was twenty-two (he was two years younger than she was) and consequently had remained that age forever, making me the only kid in the world to have a twenty-year-old grandfather with a heavy black moustache and pitch-black hair—never just hung around on scaffolding for fun, never stood there without actually building things. Her husband had learned how to be a *fravecatóre* at the tender age of eight and went on to become an excellent mason. Then, one afternoon, he fell off a tall building, not because he didn't know what he was doing but because he was exhausted, because those bums had made him work too hard. He shattered every single bone in his body, including his handsome face, which resembled my own, and blood had come gushing out of his nose and mouth. On a separate occasion, she told me that he also used to tickle her, and he did it up until the day he died, when he went off to toil forever in the hereafter, leaving her all alone on this side, without a penny, with a two-year-old little girl and a baby on the way, destined to become a person who'd never know a moment of peace. But get over here, you *scazzamaurié*, come over here to your nonna, who loves you so.

She often called me that: *scazzamauriéll*. I was her naughty but charming devil, a pain in the ass and scallywag, who chased away the nightmares and dark thoughts that overshadowed her worst days. *Scazzamaurielli*, she said, lived among the dead in that huge pit; they spent their time running around, jumping off boulders, screaming and laughing and beating each other up. Small but strong, they picked up marble shards and sharp splinters of granite and placed them in big baskets. Then, after choosing the flattest and sharpest ones, they touched them with their thick fingers to make them fiery hot and threw them like darts at the boy-ghosts and girl-ghosts that rose up from the cadavers, emanating smoke, their cruel feelings not quite ready to turn entirely to ash. Sometimes—she said quietly one day when she was particularly melancholy—the *scazzamurielli* made themselves wafer thin and squeezed past the marble cover and out of the pit, and traveled all around Naples, sneaking into the houses of the living. They chased away the crueler ghosts that lived there and brought about general good cheer. They even managed to drive off the phantasms that haunted my grandmother most, the horrifying and disrespectful ones who didn't care how weary she was, or how she'd spent her whole life sewing thousands of suede gloves for ladies, or how she now had to slave away for her daughter, son-in-law, and grandchildren, when the only person she was ever truly willing to wait on hand and foot was me.

## 3.

To be honest, I would've preferred being a poet-enchanter that could extract girlfriends from the underworld than an elfin nightmare-slayer. But at that point in time, it didn't really matter. The little ballerina who danced dangerously on the parapet didn't fall and break every bone in her body, the way my grandfather had, but hopped back down onto the balcony and ran inside, causing my heart not to jump into my throat but to land on my sleeve.

All the same, I started to worry about her. Although she hadn't fallen then, I was scared that one day she would, and consequently I didn't have much time to get to know her. So, I waited until she reappeared on the balcony and, when she did, I raised my hand in a wave, but a feeble one, so I wouldn't feel ashamed if she didn't wave back.

Which, in fact, she did not, not then and not ever, either because it was objectively hard to see my gesture or because she didn't want to give me the pleasure. Consequently, I decided to spy on the front door of her building. I hoped she'd come out alone so that I could become friends with her and talk about stuff in proper Italian, and then say: you know that if you fall, you'll die? That's how my grandfather died. It felt important to let her know that so she would have all the necessary elements to decide if she wanted to continue to expose herself to the danger or not.

For days on end, I dedicated all my free time after school and before starting my homework—time that I usually spent playing in the street, getting into fights with kids who were rowdier than me, and undertaking all sorts of dangerous challenges like doing flips over iron bars—to that goal. But she never came out, not on her own or with her parents. Clearly her life followed a different schedule, or else I was just unlucky.

But I didn't give up. I was extremely restless at that age, my head was filled with words and fantasies, all of which concerned the girl. There was no coherence to them—coherence doesn't belong to the world of children, it's an illness we contract later on, growing up. I remember wanting several things all at once. I wanted, purely by chance, to find myself standing in front of their apartment door. I would ring the bell and say to her father or mother—preferably her mother, as fathers scared me then and still do—in the language of the books that I was reading thanks to Mr. Benagosti, who lent them to me: Signora, your beloved and beautiful daughter dances so exquisitely on the parapet that I can't sleep; I am deeply concerned that she will fall to the sidewalk below, that blood will come gushing from her mouth and nose, just as it did to my grandfather, the mason. But, at the same time, I also wanted to stand at my window and wait for the girl to come back and play on her balcony so that I could show her that I wasn't afraid of risking my life either, that I could wriggle out the bathroom window, creep along the wall, and climb back in through the kitchen window, without ever looking down. I had done it twice already—it actually wasn't that hard because the two windows were connected by a narrow sill—and with a nod from her I'd happily do it a third time. If I ever did manage to talk to her, I would also tell her—because one word always leads to another—that I was in love with her beautiful soul, that my love was eternal, and that, if she really wanted to dance on the ledge and risk falling to her death, she could count on me to bring her back from the underworld, that I wouldn't stupidly turn around and look at her. Spying on her, dying in some bold act for her, or rescuing her from deep underground weren't conflicting thoughts but separate moments in a single event where, one way or another, I always came out looking good.

In the meantime, not only was I unsuccessful in making contact with her, but a long rainy spell prevented me from even watching her play on her balcony. Instead, I devoted all my energy, between one rain shower and the next, to searching for the entrance to the underworld so I wouldn't be caught unprepared in case tragedy struck. Actually, as soon as my grandmother told me about it, I started my search but without wasting too much time on it. Because of Mr. Benagosti's books, the comics my mother bought me, and the movies I saw at Cinema Stadio, I had been so busy acting out countless roles—cowboy, orphan, deckhand, shipwreck survivor, game hunter, explorer, knight errant, Hector, Ulysses, and the entire tribune of the plebes, to name just a few—that looking for the entrance to the land of the dead had become secondary. But with the girl's intrusion into my life of adventure, I redoubled my efforts and got lucky.

One afternoon when I wasn't allowed to go far from home because of the rain—*mo chiuvéva, mo schiuvéva, mo schizziàva soltanto* my grandmother said crabbily—and only down to the puddle-filled courtyard with Lello, my friend who lived in Staircase B, I discovered, just beyond the patch of grass where the palm tree stood, a rectangular slab of stone longer than I was tall, complete with a heavy chain that glistened in the rain. I froze when I saw it, and not just from the cold and damp, but out of fear.

"What's the matter?" my friend asked in alarm. I liked Lello because when there were no other kids around, he spoke in an Italian that sounded a little bit like the books I read.

"Quiet!"

"Why?"

"The dead will hear you."

"What dead?"

"All of them."

"Cut it out . . . "

"No, really. They're down there. If we can unlock the chain and lift up the rock, all the ghosts will come out."

"I don't believe you."

"Touch the chain, see what happens."

"Nothing's going to happen."

"Touch it."

Lello walked over to it while I kept my distance. He knelt down and in the very moment that he cautiously touched the chain, a blindingly bright bolt of lightning exploded in the sky, followed by heavy thunder. I fled, with Lello right behind me, ashen with fear.

"See?" I said out of breath.

"Yeah."

"Would you go down there with me?"

"No."

"What kind of friend are you?"

"There's a chain."

"We can break the chain."

"You can't break chains."

"You're just chicken. If you don't want to, I'll ask friend of mine. She's not afraid of anything."

And then something utterly mind-boggling happened.

"You mean the girl from Milan?" Lello asked with a wicked smile.

That's when I found out that the girl of my dreams had a nickname, and that I wasn't the only one who had noticed her. But there was more. Apparently, it was a well-known fact that when it was sunny, I either stood at my window ogling her or loitered outside the front door to her building. Admit it!

I retreated into my usual silence, but not before saying *vafanculostrunznunmeromperpcàzz*, the magic formula I used when no one understood just how special I was and what great things I'd go on to accomplish one day.

4.

My grandmother was the only person who really understood this, and she had known it to be true since the day I was born. As soon as I came out of her daughter's belly, she felt like life had reacquired meaning and—incredible to say and imagine today—this totally unexpected meaning was me, everything about me, including the tears, drool, vomit and shit that kept her constantly washing bibs, swaddling, and diapers.

When I was born, she was forty-five years old, and about fifty-three at the time of the events I'm recounting. She had lost all sense of joy decades earlier, and no longer expected much from life, but went on to discover all kinds of joy in me. Every single thing I did thrilled her, and not because it improved her existence, which was less than zero, no, all I had to do was bat my eyes or coo, and that blink or gurgle was proof to her that I was the greatest living organism to appear on the planet in millennia. Straight away, as soon as I was born—she used to say with so much emotion—you were a living and breathing alabaster cherub, a teaspoon of cherry syrup, a *frankfellík* of sugar, vanilla, and cinnamon; even your pee was holy water, like the time you sprayed your uncle in the face when he came over to celebrate how in nine months his sister had created something amazing out of nothing, out of the darkest shadows; he was giving you a kiss and you peed in his face! And now look at what you've become, you scallywag, you can't even sit still for a moment, come over here and let me brush your hair.

The care and devotion she showed me each and every morning was intolerable. She washed my neck and ears, parted my hair perfectly, and smoothed down any unruly locks with soap, eager to show everyone at school and the whole world just how *bellíll* I was. She doted on me and my needs far more than my brothers. It was as if she cooked just for me, blatantly expressing her preference by consistently putting the best pieces of meat on my plate. If I broke an object that was meaningful to my father, she always said it was her fault. Her conversations with her son-in-law, always full of restrained anger, went something like this:

"I did it."

"Mother-in-law, you break too many things."

"I've got butterfingers."

"Would you please be more careful?"

"Yes, of course. So sorry."

They didn't get along well, and the less they spoke, the better. My grandmother's job was to take care of the household and make sure we boys didn't misbehave, but since we always did, my father frequently got angry and scolded her. His scolding made her irritable, she'd scowl, then start muttering unkind words about him, her daughter, and my brothers. But never about me. She let me do anything, even go outside whenever I wanted. Where're you off to, little *frankellík?* Outside. Where outside? Downstairs. Come back soon. Alright, I'd say and run off.

I don't know how much time I spent in the courtyard that spring, trying to figure out how to break the chain and raise the stone slab that led, I believed, to the land of the dead. It was a cold sheet of rock, a few violets grew on either side, and now and then a cockroach crawled out from underneath. If a person were to walk casually across the courtyard, they'd only hear the sounds coming from the piazza. But if that person stood by the stone for even five minutes, like I used to, suddenly they'd hear groaning, hissing, and moaning sounds from deep underground that were terrifying. But I endured them. I was so enchanted by the number of adventures that existed for the bold—and more than anything else, I wanted to be bold, but mostly I thought I was chickenshit and wanted to change—that, at one point, in order to try and sever the chain, I even brought down my father's hacksaw, which he never let us touch out of fear that we would cut off our fingers.

I spent one whole afternoon sawing with hardly anything to show for it. I sawed and sawed but hardly nicked the chain; the only thing I managed to do was irritate the dead or the angels or the *scazzamuriéll* with the sound of metal on metal, an icy wind whipping around me, hissing, scaring me, forcing me to slow down.

My one mistake: I stayed out too long. My father came home from work, walked across the courtyard without even noticing me, and made his way upstairs. Since there was no way I could put the saw back without him seeing me, I decided to hide it in the grass. Actually, this worked out perfectly and the next day I went back to sawing the chain without subterfuges. But a sudden, loud banging noise from deep below ground—maybe an angel had caught a dead worker sneaking up toward the slab, with the goal of returning to the world of the living—scared me, and I, fed up with sawing and not getting anywhere, ran home without hiding the hacksaw.

A while later, my father came home from work angrier than ever, waving the saw in front of our faces. The caretaker of the building had found it. Is this yours, by chance? he had asked. By chance it is, my father had replied, and now he wanted to know which one of us kids had taken it and left it in the courtyard. Tears instantly sprang to my eyes—oh, how I hated that about myself, when my father got angry my eyes instantly welled with tears—and I was just about to turn myself in, sobbing, when my grandmother spoke up.

"It was me; I took it."

"You?"

"Yes."

"And why the hell did you take it?"

"I just did. I needed it."

"And you left it outside to rust, so that if I cut myself I'll die of tetanus?"

"Yes."

"Well, don't you ever forget it out there again."

That's just how she was. She'd immolate herself for me on the spot. I can't even say that I was grateful. Back then it seemed like her passion for me was just the standard torture that all grandmothers inflicted on their firstborn grandchildren, so it didn't even occur to me to say thank you. Actually, now and then, I wanted to yell, Basta! Go back to the kitchen and mind your own business, but then my mother would have slapped me, and she had endless piecework to sew and didn't want any trouble from us kids. I didn't even feel the need to reciprocate my grandmother's affection, which was gruff at times and overly sweet at others, by giving her a kiss, for example. Actually, I don't think I ever kissed my grandmother. None of us did. To tell the truth, underneath it all, I don't think I even loved her that much. Besides the fact that, objectively speaking, as far as grandmothers went, she wasn't that great; other kids had better ones.

I obtained proof of this one afternoon when a lady appeared on the girl's balcony. Dressed entirely in navy blue with pearls around her neck, she had silvery-blue hair, rosy skin, perfect posture, and played calmly with the girl until the sun went down. With the little ballerina constantly calling out Nonna, Nonna to make sure her pirouettes received the lady's full attention, I found myself thinking: now that's a nonna, and I prayed she'd never see mine, who was short and fat, hunchbacked and ugly, her ruddy cheeks marked with purplish veins, her grey hair pinned in a bun at the nape of her neck, hardly any teeth, a nose like a bell pepper and a permanently absent gaze whether cooking at the stove, washing dishes at the sink, or hunched over her knitting in a chair.

To make matters worse, while I was watching the girl and her nonna, my own grandmother stepped up behind me. What are you looking at, she asked. Nothing, I said quickly, but just then the girl tugged on her grandmother's dress and pointed directly at me, eliminating all the distance between us and practically jabbing me in the eye.

"Nothing, huh?" my grandmother said.

"Nope, nothing."

"Wave, you little liar."

"No."

"Wave, you *scazzamauriéll*. Wave, little *franfellík*."

"No."

"Then I will."

It was awful. Why, yet again, did she have to get involved in my personal business and run the risk of making me look like a fool? The thought of someone catching sight of her bothered me deeply. I didn't want the girl from Milan to see how paltry my nonna was and compare her with her own, who looked so elegant and spoke so well. I waved quickly to draw their attention onto me, but then my grandmother pushed me aside and started waving, too, mouthing the word Buongiorno, even though it was already evening. The girl and her grandmother waved back sedately, while I stomped off to the toilet, the only room where a person could find a little peace and quiet. I don't know what my grandmother did next. Maybe she stayed on at the window and continued to wave, maybe she kept mouthing words that, given the distance, they couldn't possibly hear.

## 5.

For a long time, I didn't forgive her. She was a timid woman, not at all sociable. If someone she didn't know spoke to her, she'd blush to the roots of her hair and beyond. So why had she done that? Today I realize that she went out on a limb for me because she had seen me far too many times with my face pressed up to the glass or standing at the open window in the not-quite-warm spring air, looking dejected after watching the girl for ages and getting nowhere. She had forced herself to do it out of love for me. Yes, love. No one in the course of the long arc of my life ever gave me as much love, and she kept on even after people started suspecting that Mr. Benagosti might not have been entirely right about me. Even in my first year of middle school, I had become less brilliant, I didn't understand stuff, my mind wandered; at home I was 'nzallanúto, moonstruck, the light of Selene had turned my brain to mush, as if I had aged all of a sudden. But my grandmother never gave up on me. If I seemed upset about my inadequacies and wasn't talking, not even to her, she tried to make me laugh and said things like, chiocchiò, paparacchiò, i miérgoli so' chiòchiari e tu no. What she meant was that I was unlike all the other foolish blackbirds in the world who sang the same dopey song, because I sang with an uncommon beauty that no one but her could hear. Thankfully, people like her, people who are misguided, exist. It's an enormous consolation to know that there's at least one person out there who thinks, even if they're mistaken: oh, how precious this person is to me, I'll do everything I can for them until I die. In my own life, I did it whenever I could, but the very first time was for the girl from Milan.

She, I felt, was as precious to me as I was to my grandmother. I idolized her in the same gratuitous way. How had waving benefitted my grandmother? It hadn't. When I realized the enormous effort she had made to go against her shy nature, although I may not have forgiven her, I forgot the offense and decided to love the girl in the same absolute way that my mother's mother loved me, or even more.

In the days that followed, my grandmother did everything she could to make up for it. Knowing full well she had made me unhappy, she dedicated herself to my happiness with greater discretion. For example, once, while I was trying to do some complicated math problem at the kitchen table, she came up and gently tapped me on the shoulder and said, practically in a whisper, the young lady is on the balcony now, want to see? I forgot about the math problem and ran to the window to look, while my grandmother kept on doing her chores and pretended not to notice.

Sometimes the girl from Milan played with dolls, sometimes she pretended to be a ballerina, sometimes she skipped rope in the small area between some wooden fruit crates and cleaning equipment. If she so much as glanced at me, I waved. She didn't always return the greeting, it depended how hard she was concentrating on her game, she might have waved back only when she was bored. I wonder—I thought to myself one Sunday morning when I was feeling especially lonely—if my grandmother, when she met her betrothed, was as much at sea as I was. So, I decided to ask her what had happened when they met that caused her to feel love in her chest and everywhere else.

It seemed like she didn't want to tell me, or that she didn't even know. She owned only one photo of the two of them and she protected it so jealously that even I only saw it a single time, and so quickly that I couldn't remember anything about it: two dark figures on a brownish background, they could've been anyone. When I asked her my deeply personal question, she blushed and said that when they saw each other for the very first time, they both felt as if they had warm lanterns in their hearts, and that, thanks to some marvel of illumination, possibly oil but maybe gas, their bodies were filled with light and a fire was sparked in them, oh, how beautiful it was. Because I insisted, she went on to tell me how bright and shiny his eyes were—sadly, the only light that shines now is the eternal flame in front of his burial niche at the cemetery that cost her a fortune because, and remember this Mimí, everything's for sale, you can even buy lights to illuminate the shadows of death— but that his eyes could also get icy cold, especially if someone offended him. For example, she said, every Sunday after they got married, they used to go for an afternoon stroll down the Rettifilo, and if some bastard even looked at her, Nonno would reach for his walking stick, which held a flame-bladed sword inside. This element of a stick-sword was entirely novel to me. I asked her more about it, and a conversation ensued that ended, in terms of its actual content, more or less in this way:

"Did he fight duels?"

"Oh no."

"Did he ever kill someone?"

"There was never any need."

"Was he handsome when he fought?"

"He was always handsome."

"Did he look like me?"

"Yes, but you're more handsome than he was."

"Would you marry him all over again, even if you knew he'd fall to his death?"

She didn't like that last question, it made her sad, and she stopped paying attention to me. But what else could I do? The only person willing to answer my questions on matters of Love and Death, the only person capable of giving me decent answers, was her. Now, to top things off, there was even this sword, which made the pairing of loving and dying even stronger, and at night, before falling asleep, I always thought about that walking stick. Sure, he needed to lean on it while he walked, but it also held a weapon that he could unsheathe at any moment to defend his beloved from any of the countless dangers that came at them from air or land, or even from below ground, a manly task that I considered fundamental and to which I would devote myself entirely.

Indeed, I was now in constant anxiety for the girl from Milan. I started to wave more emphatically from the window and, when she danced, I showed my admiration in an exaggerated manner. I was particularly afraid that she'd feel ignored and would climb back up onto the ledge for attention, something I didn't want her to do, and yet—I confess—I also desired. While the thought of her death was intolerable, the prospect of travelling to the underworld to bring her back was very appealing. Or, if that should never come to pass, at least spending the rest of my life lamenting—in both poetry and prose—her luminous body and the scent of spring. The idea of committing my life to this labor of love and how it would elevate me to the status of unrivaled poet moved me deeply.

## 6.

Once, upon returning home from yet another one of her tiresome errands, my grandmother even saw it fit to say: the little *signurina* is right downstairs playing hopscotch. I didn't even thank her, it was common courtesy,

after all, and she never could've resisted telling me anyway. I quit whatever homework I was doing—where are
you going? my mother yelled—and left the house without
a jacket.

I took the stairs *sciuliarèlla*-style, sliding down the dark
wooden banister. I practiced my version of it every day and
had acquired a certain flair. I didn't do it because I was in
a hurry, but simply because I liked going fast, almost lying
flat on the banister. Basically, it offered me an opportunity
to fall down the stairwell and die, and while this possibility
usually left me lukewarm at best, on this particular occasion, when I was so eager to see the girl up close, breaking
all the bones in my body seemed like something she might
appreciate.

I survived, ran across the courtyard, past the entrance to
the underworld, and burst into the piazza, my eyes darting
this way and that. But all I saw were the same old rowdy
kids doing flips around the turnstile bars near the ticket
booth, Lello zipping around on his new bike, and three or
four girls waiting their turn at the fountain, either to drink
water or rinse their hands. She wasn't there. There was so
much to see that I didn't see her.

I stopped Lello immediately. "Where's the girl from
Milan?" I yelled menacingly.

"What are you, blind?" he replied.

I looked around—a tumultuous and chaotic landscape
of walls, lampposts, shouting kids, colors both sharp and
faded, blue skies, late afternoon light—but still didn't see
her. I'm afraid that the boy I was then and the elderly man
I am today share several commonalities. When I'm looking for something now—my eyeglasses, for example—and
I feel my anxiety grow as I continue not to find them, I hear

myself say in a somewhat elevated tone of voice: I can't find anything in this house! And then my wife, frazzled by the fate that has befallen her, comes in, points to them and says: And those? What are they?

"You're the one who's blind! I can see perfectly well," I screamed at Lello.

"Oh yeah?"

Lello dropped his bike, grabbed my arm, and swearing and cussing, dragged me toward a girl playing hopscotch with other girls next to the front door of my building. I dug my heels in and resisted, but I also swept away the clouds of anxiety at not seeing her and not finding her and looked clearly. What a terrible sensation, I didn't trust myself, all it took was one mistake and I was ready to tear the whole world to shreds.

"Who's that?" Lello asked.

Even though I had never seen her up close, I was forced to admit that it was indeed the girl from Milan.

"It's her."

"What do you want with her anyway?"

"What the hell are you talking about? I wasn't looking for her."

"Liar! You came running outside screaming 'Where is she?'"

"Me? When? I didn't mean the girl; I meant the bike."

"You said the girl from Milan."

"No, I said your new bike."

To prove it, I grabbed his bike, told him I had lots of homework and not much time, but that I wanted to take a ten-minute break and play courage.

"Are you sure?"

"Yes!"

Lello didn't seem entirely convinced. He had heard me perfectly well and wanted me to admit it.

"If you came to talk to the girl from Milan, you're too late. Me and her already talked twice and pretty soon I'm going to proclaim my love for her."

I felt a deep pain in my chest and reacted without thinking. "No, you're not, you bastard. I saw her first and we've been waving at each other for a month."

"We went further. We talk to each other."

"You better not talk to her ever again."

"What if I do?"

"If you do, I'll go get my grandfather's walking stick that has a sword inside, and I'll kill you."

I was enjoying the conversation; it was almost straight out of a book. But I underestimated the effect that the walking stick would have on Lello. He forgot the girl from Milan entirely and started asking me all about the walking stick, how it was made, what kind of handle it had, if the sword was long or short, if it was flame-bladed, and most of all if I would show it to him, even from a distance. I didn't describe it in detail and didn't promise anything because, of course, not only had I never laid eyes on it, but I'd also never even seen my grandfather. I only hinted that he had been a great swordsman, and that I was, too.

"Are you ready to play courage now?" I asked, cutting the conversation short.

"Yes."

"I ride first."

"No, I do."

"I called it."

We often challenged each other to this hair-brained test of courage. We took turns: one was the cyclist and the other the pedestrian. The cyclist had to pedal as fast as he could toward the pedestrian, who had to stand as still as he could for as long as possible, waiting for the speeding bike to come rushing towards him, and then elegantly leap out of the way at the last minute. If the pedestrian stepped back too soon, it meant he was a coward.

In the meantime, I had come up with a plan. Naturally, the girl would be curious and would stop her playing to watch the heroic challenge, which, I have to say, I excelled at, both as pedestrian—I always leapt out of the way at the very last minute, because Lello, who was basically a good kid, always hit the brakes if he got too close to running me over—and as cyclist—I sped toward Lello so fast but never actually killed him because he always got scared and preferred to be considered a coward than end up having to go to the hospital. Anyway, my plan was that the girl from Milan would see how strong I was and how weak Lello was, and then she'd choose me and love me forever. With this in mind, we began.

I hopped on the bike and did a loop to pick up speed. Lello assumed the stance and waited. I focused on running him over, announcing my approach by ringing the bell and yelling wildly, so I'd also attract the attention of the girl from Milan, who I imagined was watching me and thinking with admiration, oh, I know him, that's the boy from the window, finally! As usual, Lello couldn't hold his combative stance for long, and awkwardly but wisely leapt out of the path which I, a crazed warrior on horseback, was on. I zipped past him, hit the brakes, and yelled: cowardly rogue, one day you'll pay dearly! and other such phrases. (You'll get your comeuppance was another phrase I had recently read, but it didn't sound quite right.) Unfortunately, I realized that the girl and her friends had kept on playing; even if they had glanced at me, it had had no effect whatsoever. I was filled with dismay.

I handed the bike over to Lello and got into position, my legs planted firmly and muscles tense, waiting for my buddy to come racing toward me. Lello looped around, picked up speed, and took his aim, while I yelled things like, the only way you'll win, you bastard, is over my dead body! And then just as the bike came barreling down, bell ringing wildly, I realized—with amazement—that the girl was watching me, maybe she was trying to understand what kind of idiotic game we were playing, or maybe she was afraid for my life and was already contemplating traveling to the underworld in my place, oh, how electrifying it was to think that she was worried about my well-being the same way I worried night and day about hers.

It was so electrifying that I didn't jump out of the way. Lello, shocked by the absurdity of my excessive audacity, jammed on the brakes only at the very last second, but not before running over my left foot with the front wheel and shredding my bare ankle with the mudguard and tire tread.

## 7.

During that phase of my life, I was increasingly bothered that I was still a child, and yet I couldn't quite stop being one. When it came to the question of losing my life, I was more or less at an impasse: perishing heroically in the course of a war, earthquake, tidal wave, outbreak of yellow fever, fire, or in the collapse of a mine with the inevitable methane leak, while imagining very normal deaths for my family members, seemed a high point in my management of life's pleasures and sorrows. It only needed a little exaggeration to say that it gave me joy; but if I got a scratch or felt pain or saw blood, then life was intolerable, and even worse if accompanied by a few humiliating sniffles and tears, and the possibility that I might later speak of the incident as some mortal wound offered no consolation at all. In this, too, the elderly man I am now resembles the child I was then. While I was terrified of death in the prime of my life, I don't care about it at all now, but surgeries or any intrusive scientific procedures focused on exploring, removing, and suturing, followed by the agony of awakening post-anesthesia with pain, despair, and wounds that need cleaning, feeling battered, mentally fatigued and imagining the moment of passing away, now that scares me, that scares me so much that even seventy years on, I may well start to cry like I did when I was nine.

When Lello came crashing into me, the level of chaos that exploded—I was standing, I had fallen down, I couldn't think straight, had the asphalt given way? Was I falling?—was so intense that the tears and pain ended up getting tucked away deep inside my brain tissue somewhere. The only thing I remember was how Lello threw down his bike and started shouting, and not in our usual Italian way. He said things like *nunnècolpamia, aggiofrenato, tesífattomale, fammevedé, omaronnamia.* When I realized I was lying flat on the ground, I sat up in a hurry. I couldn't have that. I felt pain around my ankle and glanced down apprehensively. It was nothing, just a strip of red. I reached out to examine it delicately, which led to the fatal blow. When I touched my skin, the red strip turned much redder, as if my fingers had lacerated it, and all of a sudden blood started to flow. I felt lost, a bunch of kids were standing around, I hoped that the girl from Milan wasn't one of them. Oh, how brusquely desire fluctuates. All I wanted to do was cry and wail without having to worry about impressing her or coming across as brave. It didn't help that Lello kept pointing at my wound and saying *tèsciosàng*, something from inside moving out, as if part of me was escaping me, clouding my vision and making me want to lie down and shut my eyes once and for all.

Instead, I did the opposite. I forced myself to stand up, rubbed my eyes as if to see better, and, limping heavily, made my way toward the fountain with my head hung low. I didn't want to see or talk to anyone—a lot of the kids had already gone back to their games, muttering *nunsè-fatteniént*—actually, I was so irate that I wished I had my grandfather's walking stick so that I could windmill the flaming sword above my head and take my revenge on everyone around me who was unharmed, while I had been wounded so badly. Lello went back to speaking in proper Italian.

"Here, lean on me."

"I don't need you, you bastard. Look what you did to me."

"I'll come with you."

"No, don't. Better alone than in bad company."

I hobbled off, eyes downcast, trailing my wounded leg toward the fountain. I rinsed it with maniacal care and muted groans. The more I checked to see if blood was streaming, dripping, or if there was any blood at all—by then it had almost stopped and it burned, but it was nothing to scream and writhe over—the more I saw myself falling victim to anemia—that lurking beast we kept away by consuming the occasional serving of much-reviled and very bloody horse meat—or tetanus, that other mysterious word that could mean earthworm as easily as it could mean snake, an illness my excellent father dreaded we kids would contract as soon as we skinned a knee or got the smallest of cuts.

So, there I was at the fountain, splashing water on my wound, when all of a sudden, I heard a gentle voice—a sound I have never forgotten—say: can I take a sip? The accent was clearly foreign. No one from Naples, not even Lello, spoke Italian like that. I instantly pulled my bare foot and ankle out of the water, it was all too much, so many emotions, so much courage, danger, and blood, the huge effort it took to be masculine and strong and not cry, and now her, here she was, the girl from Milan, asking me, can I take a sip? I replied grimly, gruffly: yes, and I took a step back.

The jet of water from the fountain fell strong and hard, a white needle, ending in a monotonous gurgle in a basin of dirty foam, leaves, pebbles, rubble, bits of paper. The girl leaned forward, draped her arm around the metal structure, and lowered her head to drink. I realized that she didn't have braids like Lizzie, the sister of Kit, the hero of *The Little Sheriff*, nor did she have long, flowing hair like Flossie, Kit's girlfriend. Someone had cut her hair short, maybe in view of the oncoming hot weather. Everything about her was dark: her hair and eyebrows, her skin from playing in the sun on the balcony, her eyes. But when she opened her mouth to drink, her teeth were so white and straight that they've continued to shine in my memory my whole life. The water splashed across her lips and dripped down her chin while she peered at me closely, a hint of either mischief or curiosity in her eyes. She must've been very thirsty because she drank for what seemed a very long time, but as far as I was concerned, she could have drunk all the water in the fountain and never move again, she was so beautiful to watch. Eventually though, she stopped drinking, the water went back to its monotonous gurgle, and she turned to me.

"Did you hurt yourself?"

"No."

"You're bleeding."

"Just a little."

"Can you show me?"

I nodded. She leaned over, hands on her knees.

"There's blood," she said and touched the wound with the tip of her right index finger.

I repressed an ouch and thinking it was the right thing to do, I said, "I like it when you dance like a wind-up ballerina."

"Me too."

"I like it more. But don't fall."

"I won't."

"If you do, though, I'll save you."

"Thank you."

We stayed there on our own, inside a compact cluster of things and minutes, the fountain gurgling in the background and us chatting in the way I've attempted to describe. And then, out of nowhere, a fat, blond woman came storming over and grabbed the girl by the arm and started scolding her in the very same Neapolitan that we spoke at home, which was entirely unlike the girl's way of speaking: *cchitaratoperméss, eh, mestaifacènnascípazz, taggiocercatadapertútt, macómm, tujescecàsasènzadicereniént, moverímmoquannetòrnanomammepapà, moverímm.* And she whisked her away, leaving me both overjoyed and in total despair.

## 8.

My wound was disinfected by my mother, anxiously examined for tetanus by my father, and ignored by my grandmother, who suffered so deeply when I injured myself that she cast her eyes downward and focused on her household chores, her lips occasionally moving without emitting sound, maybe praying or maybe cursing her misfortune. I whined a little at how the spirit alcohol burned, but when it wasn't used to disinfect wounds, I loved the way its odor made me go weak at the knees, its connection to ghosts, and how it was used to preserve cherries. As I recall, I immediately forgot the wound; I was anesthetized by love.

This marked the beginning of a period of joyful trepidation. I couldn't wait to talk to the girl from Milan again. Exchanging glances from window to balcony was no longer enough. The day after getting wounded, I waited for her to reappear on her balcony, but she did not. I went down to the fountain at around the same time, hoping to find her sipping water and talking, pronouncing each and every word in her melodious way. Instead, I bumped into Lello.

He looked at my ankle and sighed with relief. "Oh, it's nothing," he said.

"I lost at least two pints of blood."

"But you're fine."

"Not really."

"What did the girl from Milan say to you?"

"None of your business."

"Actually, it is—I want to marry her."

We argued at length and decided to resolve the matter with a duel to the death, to be held in the courtyard near the entrance to the underworld. We discussed the weapons we'd use. I was in favor of using the metal ribs from an umbrella that we had previously hidden in the cellar. He opposed the idea and insisted that I fight with my grandfather's walking stick. I objected, saying that if he dueled with a simple metal rib and I with the flaming sword, I'd have an unfair advantage and would definitely kill him. This didn't bother him. He was so curious to see the walking stick that he was willing to die. Actually, he was so insistent we had to delay the duel, even though I urgently needed to kill him.

I puzzled over what to do. Although practically every day was sunny by then, the girl never returned to the piazza to play on her own, and seldom appeared on the balcony. When she did appear, I ran and shut myself in the bathroom, looked out the small window, watched her, waved to her, and sometimes even dangled my wounded leg out the window so she could see it. While I can't say that she responded enthusiastically to my calls for attention, she was curious and occasionally waved back. Unfortunately, no other kind of communication was possible. We couldn't yell back and forth because everyone at home and out on the street would've heard me, and also because her mother and father—an elegant Milanese couple, though my mother and even my father were better-looking—often came out onto the balcony to check on her, as did the fat Neapolitan-speaking witch who had stolen her away from me.

My head was on fire. I couldn't forget how the water glistened on her lips and white teeth. Before falling asleep, I used to imagine climbing the drainpipe up to her balcony, except there was no drainpipe. Or else I'd imagine swinging from my bathroom window to her balcony on a rope, from my shady area to her sunny one. I was restless and thought, with a combination of concern and conceit, that my restlessness was proof of my exceptional nature. Only much later did I realize that this kind of *pazzaría* is typical of men of all ages when they put women at the top of their list of *pazzièlle*.

At one point, it seemed like a good idea to send the girl from Milan a message that said something like: I beseech you, don't talk to Lello, speak only to me. Initially I thought I'd write it in giant letters on a piece of paper torn from the big roll that my father used for sketching, but in the end, I decided that wasn't such a good idea. It wasn't safe, the whole neighborhood would see it. After much hesitation, I decided in favor of the trusty red mailbox in the piazza, which I had used in the past to send my lyrical verses to both the living and the dead. It didn't cost a thing, all I had to do was make sure no one was around, climb onto a low wall, reach all the way over, and slip my piece of notebook paper inside, but not without first drawing a stamp on it. Usually, my letters didn't have a clear recipient—I sent both prose and poems to the entire human race. But on that particular occasion, at the top of the page I wrote: for the girl from Milan. I drew a stamp on it and colored it in, and finally, in my very best penmanship, which sometimes earned Mr. Benagosti's praise, I wrote out the message I had already composed—I beseech you, don't talk to Lello, speak only to me—and then I topped it off with:

I'm a whole lot stronger and a whole lot better looking. Stunned by the pleasurable experience of writing that missive, I made my way to the mailbox, and had just dropped it in when Lello came up behind me.

"What did you just put in there?"

"What's it to you?"

"Tell me."

"A letter from my father to Mané, the painter. Ever heard of him?"

"No."

"See? You can't marry the girl from Milan because you don't know anything!"

"People get married even if they don't know the names of painters."

"Not with the girl from Milan."

"She'll decide who she wants to marry."

"The sword will decide. First, I'll kill you and then I'll make her mine."

"Fine. But only if you bring your grandfather's walking stick."

He was obsessed with that thing. It was then, I think, that I decided to construct, together with my brother who was good at building things, a walking stick whose pommel doubled as a handle that you could tug on and pull out one of my grandmother's knitting needles, which in terms of a sword, was much more realistic than an umbrella rod. Here it is, I'd say to Lello. And then: *en garde.* This would be followed by a long and dangerous swordfight, leading—I hoped—to Lello's death. In a pool of blood, of course.

## 9.

Anything I have ever invented, ever since I was small, always required a pinch of truth. I needed to see the old photograph of my grandfather and grandmother again, as my memory of it had faded. If I wanted to make a convincing replica of the walking stick I needed to take a look at the real one, and I hoped the weapon was visible in the photo. I started to pester my grandmother, masking my urgency to study the walking stick as a grandson's affection for his grandfather. She blushed more than usual, hemmed and hawed, and said that I would have to wait. I understood she needed to find just the right moment, and this moment—I intuited—was not only when my father wasn't home but when she was certain he wouldn't be back anytime soon.

She didn't want to be subjected to the sarcastic tone he took with her—which sometimes became downright insulting—when he talked about her distant past as someone's darling, fiancée, wife. Mother-in-law—he'd say when he was in a good mood—go on, tell us the truth, you don't even remember what happened, it was so long ago. Were you sleeping? Were you awake? Maybe you were just lying there, and along came this gent, all dressed to the nines, and bam-bam-bam, just like that, two children were born, one that's beautiful, thank goodness, but the other one ugly and dumb, just like your husband, the mason, may his soul rest in peace. But what can you do? Kids take after their parents, and your son turned out to be such a stingy bastard that he has never, not once, given me a penny to help out with everything you cost me, so if you're living here, like some fancy lady, it's all thanks to me and my generosity as a great artist, and that's just the way things are. Oh stop, stop your crying now, mother-in-law, don't get angry, you know I'm just teasing, you know I respect you.

More or less that's what he said, but my grandmother didn't like that kind of joking around, didn't like it at all; it offended her deeply and made her angry. She bit her lip, fought back the tears, and hid her feelings and possessions in a dark wooden box under her bed so he couldn't see them or speak about them any more than he already did.

Since I often hid from my father, too, I understood perfectly. Her box of secrets was not that different from my secretive games and fantasies, which I interrupted or banished from my thoughts entirely when he came home like some black-feathered angel from the land of the dead. So, I pestered her to show me the photo when my father wasn't around and when I was certain he'd be gone for a few hours. I insisted so much that she finally gave in. She got down on her knees, pulled the box out from the dark recesses under her bed, rustled around in it, found the photo, pushed the box back into the shadows, and got to her feet with a groan.

I need to underscore what a critical moment in my childhood this was, and yet it does not possess a specific space, mood, or light, it is not imbued with the warmth or sound of my grandmother's breathing. In my memory I see only the photo: a rectangular piece of brownish cardboard, the image marked with several white cracks. Nothing else, not even me. I can only presume that my gaze went directly to my grandfather, the man who would one day fall and shatter all his bones; he stood behind a chair, one elbow resting on it, leaning slightly forward, his shiny dark hair was slicked back, revealing not an excessively wide forehead but not a small one either, heavy and dusky eyebrows, kind eyes, his white shirt contrasting sharply with his dark suit, a short striped tie held in place with a clip made from some precious metal, a breast pocket handkerchief, and finally, there it was, the awe-inspiring walking stick.

He really had it with him, a black wooden walking stick with a handle that could've been silver. But he wasn't leaning on it, which would've been the natural thing to do. No, he was holding the cane with two hands in front of his chest on a slight diagonal. He's holding it like that, I thought to myself, so that if someone like my father says something offensive, he'll tighten his grip on the sheathe with his left hand and extract the sword with his right. I could already see my grandfather coming back from the dead to stab his son-in-law for being so disrespectful to the woman he had married. It was his duty. The whole world, every single existence, orbited around this cruel battle. In one way or another, we men were forced to live in a constant state of alert, we had to be ready to fight or fight back, to be wronged so that we could get revenge, or to instigate wrongs ourselves and thereby crush all potential avengers. Yes, that was our destiny, and nothing could silence us, not even death. On the contrary. With both elegance and rage, my young grandfather leapt off the cardboard, took out the sword, brandished it over his head, and then pointed it at me, playfully inviting me to a duel.

"He was good looking, wasn't he?" my grandmother asked me softly, her voice cracking with emotion.

"Yes."

"What about me?"

Only then, and because of her question, did I realize that she was there, too. I glanced casually back at the photo. There she was, sitting in the chair—or maybe it was the throne of a princess—on which the young man with the walking stick leaned. She was the tremendous surprise. She was draped in jewels, and now owned none: pendant earrings heavy with precious stones, a diamond brooch in the shape of a small shooting star, a golden necklace with a cross, a long shiny *chiacchiere* chain with a watch attached to it that rested in her lap, a bracelet, and at least three rings—two on one hand, one on the other. She sat enveloped in a long dress that went all the way down to her shoes, with fabric falling loosely over her crossed legs but tight at the waist and on her chest— where it was decorated with buttons, pleats, ruffles and puffy sleeves—the color of the fabric was hard to identify, brown like the photo and scratched with white rivulets. Extending upwards out of the dress was her long, straight neck, at the top of which—to my amazement—was a co- rolla of hair: masses of soft, dark ringlets and waves, held in place with endless numbers of hairpins and combs. And finally, her face. Oh, how delicate her face was, the shape of her eyes, her cheekbones, the form of her mouth. She was looking straight at me, and I thought: no, it can't be, and I had some kind of seizure.

"And me?" my grandmother asked again, apprehen- sively. "What about me?"

"So beautiful," I replied.

And it was true, she was really beautiful, but for the first time in my life I realized that sometimes words were like those toys with mechanisms inside that suddenly stopped working. What did she want to know? What had I told her? Was she asking about herself now? She had said, And me? but did she mean now? In the photo or out of it? When and for whom? Was she referring to the grandmother who was showing me the photo or to the one in the photo standing next to the dead man with his walking stick? My imagination spun out of control. It occurred to me that if the marvelous lady in the photo was truly my grandmother, she must have died from sorrow along with her husband, the mason, and therefore the horribly ugly grandmother by my side must be some kind of rare species of living grandmother that had, however, died many years earlier; or maybe the beautiful lady had generously descended into the underworld to bring back her husband but then had turned around to look at him, lost him, and returned to the world of the living blighted by that awful experience. It was too bad, really, because if she had stayed the way she was in the photograph, the grandmother of the girl from Milan would've been no match for her, I would've kept calling her over to the window and showing her off to the girl, and, at the first chance I got, maybe even by the fountain, after she'd had her sip of water, I would've said to her, you're even prettier than my grandmother, who, as you've seen, is a whole lot prettier than yours.


## 10.


Thanks to my brother, who was two years younger but far cleverer and more skillful, two walking sticks were produced out of nothing. They were made from cardboard, painted black, and just hollow enough to hold a knitting needle, the dull end of which was firmly affixed to the light grey wooden handle, which gleamed like silver in the sunlight. We tried them out to see how they well they worked for dueling and discovered they were amazing. To complete the job, I asked my brother to file down the tip of Lello's sword so it was blunt and sharpen mine. He did both jobs to perfection.

There then followed a long series of negotiations with my friend, who didn't entirely trust me.

"Will you bring the walking stick?" he asked.

"I'll bring two," I said.

"I don't believe you."

"I'll show you tomorrow."

"Tomorrow I have something to do."

"Then the day after tomorrow."

"I don't know . . ."

"Are you chicken?"

"You're the one who's chicken."

"You've gone pale, you're scared you're going die!"

"I couldn't care less about dying."

"Sure, right."

"Anyway, even if I die, I'll still marry the girl from Milan."

"You can't get married if you're dead!"

"We'll see about that."

"What are you talking about? You just can't!"

It was annoying how Lello continued to talk about marrying her even if he died. Eventually, I found a way of getting to him.

"You're no fun," I said.

"Yes, I am," he retorted.

"I swear I'm never going to play with you again," I said and started to leave.

He came running after me. "Fine, tomorrow, four o'clock in the afternoon."

"Forget it, I don't want to play with someone who's no fun."

"I'm more fun than you."

"Fine, but these are the rules: if you die, I get to marry the girl from Milan."

"Fine. Bring the walking sticks."

We were supposed to meet at the stone entrance to the underworld, but just before I snuck out of the house with my brother, who insisted on being the one to carry the prodigious weapons of his creation, something entirely unexpected happened. I peeked out the window and saw the girl on the balcony doing something I hadn't seen her do in a long time: dancing. I hesitated. What to do? Should I back out of the duel, to be forever labeled a coward, and not take my eyes off her so she would know she was the center of all my thoughts? Or, should I run and fight the duel the way I felt I must, and leave her on her own, running the risk that she would feel abandoned and neglected and quite possibly so unhappy that she might climb up on the ledge and dance dangerously close to the abyss?

For one long minute, love and violence raged within. She kept on dancing, her pirouettes both holding me back and compelling me to run down to the courtyard so that I could test out—in a battle to the death with Lello, the rival who wanted to sully her—the weapons crafted by my brother. Today, my grandchildren kill and are killed in intense games of virtual reality. We used to pretend to kill and get killed on the floors of our homes, out on the street, and in the courtyards of our buildings in a dangerous blur of reality and fiction, where, if we opened the wrong door or went down the wrong alley, we could have easily found ourselves face-to-face with actual weapons. I watched the girl dance in the sunlight, her movements so graceful and sweet that I wished I could reach all the way over and touch that sweetness, then lick my fingers as if I'd touched cotton candy. I had an idea: why duel in the courtyard near the entrance to the underworld? Why not kill Lello, after a long and arduous battle, out in the street, under the girl's balcony?

My brother and I hurried to the meeting place. Lello was already waiting impatiently next to the stone slab.

"Where's the walking stick?"

"We brought two so that our duel will be fair."

My brother showed him the two sticks. Lello examined them and started to complain, they weren't what he expected. My brother was offended. Look carefully, you bastard, he said, they're tons better than any other stick-swords out there. He showed Lello how to pull out the swords, how well-crafted the handle was, how lifelike the blades were. Lello's jaw dropped, he had to admit he'd never seen anything like them. I interrupted the conversation.

"I'm in a hurry. If you don't want to duel with me, I'll find someone else."

"Fine, let's do it."

"Not here."

"Where?"

"Under the balcony of the girl from Milan."

"That's where you want to die?"

"Yes."

"Fine, let's go."

We ran out into the piazza, took a sharp right, and then turned right again. What an amazing afternoon that was. We arrived out of breath, Lello shouting to attract the girl's attention, me a few feet behind, shouting even more loudly, and my brother—who carried the weapons to make sure that they didn't get damaged—following in silence. Would she or wouldn't she look down, I wondered nervously, and I hoped she would, and Lello probably did, too. My brother handed us the weapons, Lello extracted his sword and assumed the pose of a great fencer, while I pulled out mine to make sure it was the sharp one. It was, I had the right sword, I knew I could count on my brother. But I was even more pleased when I realized that she was coming into view over the parapet of her third-floor balcony: first her face, then her shoulders, and finally her whole torso. One thing was for sure, when it came to danger, she didn't fool around, despite being a girl. She had climbed up onto something to watch. She was leaning out to see what I was doing; it didn't occur to me for a second that she might be wondering about Lello. She was truly splendid, a reflection of light shone above her head like a small flame. I lunged at Lello without the usual formal salute, something we both knew how to do well, so that he wouldn't notice her. And with this rude gesture, our duel began.

It was a long battle, at least in my memory, which houses our earliest narratives, the emotional and deceptive ones we like to call memories or recollections. In actual fact, I can't be certain. It probably lasted just long enough for us to imagine ourselves Robin Hood, the king's musketeers, or French paladins fighting for the exclusive attention of queens, princesses, and just, in general, girls, who were like hidden treasures that we were willing to lay down our lives to protect. I believe that for the duration of the duel I called out fencing terms that I had read in a battered old book that my grandmother's sister's husband, a carabiniere, had once given me, in a kind of running commentary: *doublé, coup d'estoc, inquartata, tocco, affondo.* Words that did not correspond to reality, of course. I'd never dueled before, never fenced, nothing, it was all just talk. Then I noticed that the girl was moving, she had clambered onto the parapet, and was getting to her feet. Apparently, she had gotten bored of watching and wanted some attention. I continued to lunge and strike but in silence, watching her out of the corner of my eye and thinking, when she falls, I'll rush over and catch her in my arms. But then, just as she started to dance, I realized that I was jabbing at empty air. Lello had momentarily lowered his sword—the tip was touching the sidewalk—and stood watching the girl from Milan like an idiot, his torso so ridiculously exposed to my sword that I found myself furiously thinking, he's more in love with her than I am. All it took was a fraction of a second. The fat woman burst onto the balcony, grabbed the girl, and started screaming, What are you trying to do? Kill me? And she dragged the girl back inside, continuing to yell *tummevuofàmuríammé!* This was followed by my grandmother sticking her head out the window and shouting: who gave you boys permission to go downstairs? Get up here right now! I glared at Lello with jealousy and jabbed the knitting needle in his arm.

## 11.

Because, around that time, I had managed to transform even blood—especially the blood of others—into something fictional, I didn't cry, nor did I get scared. Lello, on the other hand, screamed out in pain, burst into tears, and terrified my brother, who promptly gathered up the swords and went home. I tried to examine my enemy's wound, but he pulled his arm away. *Strunzguardachemmefàtto*, he shouted in Neapolitan. What about what you did to me? I rebutted, reminding him of how he had flayed my ankle with his bike, and I hadn't said a thing, not even a whisper, I had simply walked over to the fountain and rinsed it off. Come on, I said, don't cry, I'll help you rinse it off, what kind of man are you? To prove to me that he was indeed a man, and not a little girl, Lello forced himself to stop crying, came to the fountain with me, and stuck his arm under the jet of water. But when he saw the wound, he started crying again. I got scared, ditched him, and ran home.

All sorts of trouble ensued, too much to even list. Basically, I had to face my mother, my father, Lello's mother, Lello's father, and even Lello's older brother, who kicked me, punched me, and threw rocks at me. My grandmother was the only person who took my side, and she even tried to suggest that it was all my brother's fault, that he was the one who had stolen the knitting needles, constructed the swords, and led me down that troubled path, that I simply wasn't capable of such things. The only time she got upset was when I reminded her that even Nonno had taken part in duels: what was so bad about dueling? It was normal. Your nonno never took part in any duels, she murmured, and then stopped talking for I don't remember how long.

I quickly forgot everything and so did Lello. Soon we went back to our friendly rivalry. Actually, he was the one who told me that the girl from Milan had left for something called *villeggiatura*, but that she'd be back at the end of the summer, when we could try and kill each other again for her. Then he showed me all the messages I had put in the mailbox. They had been arranged in order and placed on a low wall with a rock on top to keep them from blowing away. The mailman, who had read them, had not only left a few comments of Bravo! here and there, he had also corrected my spelling mistakes.

"You don't even know how to spell properly in Italian," Lello said smugly.

"I know how to write better than you," I replied.

"No, you don't. You make spelling mistakes, and I don't."

"I only make a few."

"I don't make any," Lello said.

"You're lying! *Buciardo!*"

"You want to bet? Spell that!"

"What? *Buciardo?*"

"Yes."

"B-u-c-i-a-r-d-o."

"Wrong. It's with a -g, not a -c. It's *bugiardo*."

"Who says?"

"The dictionary, that's who. You want to write poems . . . but you don't even know how to spell!"

I walked off clutching my letters and feeling depressed, firstly because I had never seen a dictionary since we didn't have one at home; secondly because the mailbox had lost all its magic and turned out to be, like so many other things in this world, nothing more than a bright red metal box;

thirdly because my message for the girl from Milan had evidently never reached its destination. And so, I decided that when she came back from *villeggiatura*, I would somehow overcome all the obstacles that stood between us and, face to face, hand her all the poems that I had ever written and would continue to write for her. In the meantime, I devoted myself to a series of activities designed to speed up the summer. I fought battles with Lello and read all the comics he owned and lent me, I practiced doing flips over the bars, and I collected leaves and examined how beautiful and firm they were at first, but then how, after some time, they shriveled up and crumbled at the touch.

More than anything else, I studied my grandmother. Now that I had seen her photograph, it was clear to me that the young man with the sword in his walking stick had taken one look at her and fallen in love at least as much as I had with the girl from Milan. I had no doubt that if the grandmother from the photograph were to step off that brownish cardboard and walk into the kitchen, I could fall in love with her, and, if she'd have me, even marry her and be photographed with her, carrying my very own weapon. But what was the connection between that grandmother and the one that lived with us? Nothing. Once or twice, I made her swear that it really was her in the photograph, and even though she did, I still couldn't find a link between the two of them, and I was certain she'd never lie under oath, at least not to me. It was her transformation that created all the problems. Sure, I had seen photos of my mother, but she was only mediocre in them while in real life she was gorgeous. What was I supposed to think? Would my mother undergo the same horrible transformation that my grandmother had? What about the girl from

Milan? What an awful conundrum—I thought to myself while examining my collection of leaves—its solution definitely had something to do with death. Maybe my beautiful grandmother had, out of love, gone to toil alongside her young husband in the land of the dead under the command of the black-feathered angels. Maybe she had left an ugly grandmother in her place, I continued to hypothesize, one that was ready to shrivel up and crumble like the leaves I picked off trees and bushes. And so, sometimes, while pretending to be the great poet Orpheus intent on saving Eurydice and wandering around that hidden corner of the courtyard where the entrance to the underworld lay, I told myself that if that stone slab really did cover the entrance to the land of the dead and if I actually did manage to break through the chain, maybe I could pull out my grandmother, the one from the photograph, and even my young grandfather, and, in exchange, give the angels the grandmother we had at home, since she was a hard worker and therefore better suited to slogging away in the darkness.

I often tried to include Lello in my adventures over the course of that summer, but with little success. I wanted him to play the part of the reliable sidekick and die so that I could go and fight off the dark angels and bring him back to life before the worms devoured him. But not long after getting wounded, Lello had a growth spurt and became increasingly skeptical of my stories, which consequently made me start to doubt them, too. Even when I told them to myself, I'd soon get bored and even a little embarrassed. In all of July and August, I managed to drag him over to the entrance to the underworld only twice. The first time it was pretty fun, but the second time, in part because I started talking about the black-feathered angels, and in part because I tried to convince him that the sounds coming from underground were actually my grandfather shouting for help to get out, he got fed up. You're an idiot, he said and walked off.

Summer came to an end with me feeling lonely and thinking, as I continued to spy on the girl's still-empty balcony, that Lello was probably right, I was an idiot. Maybe even my grandmother, to her great dismay, had started thinking the same thing because she soon stopped fussing over me and if she saw me staring out the window, she scowled more than usual and exchanged worried looks with my mother, who said things to me like: look, I bought you *Tex*, and even *The Little Sherriff*, go on, go read them. I read Tex and I read Kit, but at the appearance of either Lizzie with her braids or Flossie without, I went back to staring out the window.

In early September, I bumped into Lello.

"So, when does this *villeggiatura* thing end?" I asked him.

"What *villeggiatura*?"

"The one that the girl from Milan is on."

"You're still thinking about the girl from Milan?"

"Why, you're not?"

"I can't believe you haven't heard."

"Haven't heard what?"

"The sea was rough and the girl from Milan drowned."

My reaction to the news was excessive: I lost all sensation in my legs; they gave out entirely. I could only feel my torso and head. It was an entirely new physical experience. My vision went cloudy. I was overcome with the same revulsion I felt whenever I saw a bit of parsley on a plate, the way it looked like a dead fly. I fainted, collapsing first onto Lello and then to the ground.

I got back up with my friend's help. He didn't seem overly concerned. He had an older sister who often fainted. "Men don't faint. You're a girl," he said.

## 12.

I don't remember much talk about the death of the girl from Milan, I only remember what Lello said, nothing else, not before or after. Sometimes I heard her calling out short phrases to me in her pretty way and I'd go to the window, but no one ever appeared on that third-floor balcony.

It started to rain, I remember that. I had always liked rain. It fell heavily on the balcony, now black with grime, and the wind blew away all the white, red, and pink flower petals. Rain dripped from windowsills and flowed down sidewalks, carrying leaves and litter into the street drains. I was mesmerized by the drops that formed on my grandmother's laundry line, each one so pure, and I observed them as they slowly detached, gripping the line to the bitter end with their liquid hands.

I entirely forgot my plan to go and retrieve the girl, should she die, from the great beyond. It wasn't that I didn't care or because I was insensitive, but due to poor health. After receiving the news from Lello and then fainting, I had a run of fevers that my grandmother claimed were related to growing. I recall nightmares in which I killed black-feathered angels, deftly wielding my grandfather's sword. Often, while delirious, I watched in ecstasy as the girl from Milan drank from the fountain, but suddenly the water would transform into stormy seas with huge, yellowish waves that came crashing down under a sand-colored sky. I grew especially disturbed when I saw that she had become as diaphanous as certain clouds. Seeing her like that crushed me so hard that I, myself, felt practically transparent, and this scared me.

The growing fevers went on for months. I'd get better, go back to school, and then get sick again, but mostly I was always irritable and distracted. Every so often I'd look out at the balcony and notice that something was gone: the old fruit crates, the cleaning tools, a yellow cabinet. Eventually that empty space, which had once been filled with gracious movements and dance steps, although exposed and uncovered, seemed to be bleaker and more frightening than the pit of the dead. In much the same way, the stone slab in the courtyard gradually stopped scaring me. The last time I went to examine it, something slammed up against the rock from deep down inside. A violent blow caused the chain to reverberate, but I wasn't the slightest bit spooked. I waited to see if anything else happened, it didn't, and so I went back inside.

This was followed by an incredibly long period during which, one day, I'd remember the box underneath my grandmother's bed; another day, I'd remember not only my grandfather's walking stick but everything about his clothes, his short tie, shirt, breast pocket handkerchief; yet another day and with no apparent link, I'd recall a white dress that the girl from Milan wore in the sunshine, or a delicate chain I noticed around her neck while she was drinking from the fountain.

Once, I asked my grandmother to show me everything she had saved that had belonged to her husband. Because the fevers were making me grow so tall—soon I'd reach the ceiling, she said—she didn't refuse, and showed me everything immediately. That's how I discovered that there was nothing particularly memorable inside the box, only some old photographs of her sisters, a few documents of little interest to me, and the tiepin that my grandfather was wearing in the single brownish photograph they had together, which wasn't even gold. I asked her about Nonno's things: his trousers, jacket, shirt, shoes, socks, underwear, his mason's tools, the walking stick. Where were they all now? She got flustered and thought I was accusing her of some crime that was inconceivable to both her and me. She went pale and didn't reply, I got angry at her for not caring about the things he had possessed and which, in some way, possessed him, the man standing next to her, before ending up deep underground, exposed to the wind and rain in the pit of the dead. Did you throw them out? Did you give them away? Did you sell them? I asked in rising hostility. I know now that I caused her great suffering, but back then I didn't care. For a long time, I was filled only with rage. I thought about the girl's balcony and her dolls, her closed shoes and open-toed sandals, her dresses and camisoles and the ribbons she'd used to tie her braids, all those belongings that had been left empty, or devoid of her touch and scent, and which had probably all been given away.

I decided then that for as long as I lived, I would never again buy a single thing, even if I outgrew my clothes. My coat had become tight at the shoulders and my sleeves were ever shorter, but I didn't care, I'd wear out my clothes until they were tattered shreds. After all, what was the point of washing, putting on fancy clothes, getting all dressed up if one day you go off to do your job as a mason and fall to your death, or you go on vacation one summer and drown? I wanted to devote my life to deterioration, but my grandmother, in her annoying way, kept ignoring my brothers and favoring me in everything. She'd say to my mother and father, but more as a general statement: *chistuguagliónenunpoghíascòlaccussí*. She wanted them to buy me new shoes or take me to the barber because my hair was too long, too messy. My parents pretended not to hear, they didn't have enough money, and I was fine with wearing out my clothes. I wanted everything to unravel and fray, including my body.

### 13.

I even eroded, intentionally, I think, my reputation as a good student. As early as middle school, I started feeling proud of my bad grades. It was as if disappointing Mr. Benagosti's predictions brought me pleasure, for he had been a bit too vague. Who knew just how long it would take for his prophecy to come true. In the meantime, the great adventures that awaited me grew ever vaguer. Without even realizing it, I had gone from wanting to be a knight to an explorer of the North and South poles to a missionary, so I could devote my life to the destitute of the world. I was fed up: why bother preserving myself under spirit alcohol for situations that I figured would never come to pass.

In the meantime, the balcony had filled up with new tenants, all boys, of no interest to me whatsoever. Not long after, we left that house with its view from the windows and moved to a different place with different views. I started observing new things and fell in love often. But I continued to shuffle along sloppily, indifferent about everything, whether friends or school, and roaming the city streets on my vacations. Love would suddenly blaze up inside only to quickly fade away. Often its sole purpose was to inspire poems and stories.

In fact, for whatever mysterious reason, writing seemed to be the only thing I could leave behind after my death that didn't seem like a waste. I wrote half-hearted poems and simple stories about the desire to perish before the failures and delusions of life led to my inevitable deterioration. The result was generally despairing, which to my mind meant good. I kept my pages of writing in a tin container which, like my grandmother, I hid under my bed. I was concerned that my father would read them and discover my shortcomings as a poet and storyteller, in addition to my spelling, grammar, and syntactical mistakes, and humiliate me.

Years went by in this way. Although writing "years went by in this way" might seem like a shortcut, it's exactly what happened. The years went by in one big compact block, with me doing and thinking the same things over and over, or at least that's how it felt. All in all, only a couple of relevant events stood out. When I was sixteen, I argued with my Italian professor when he gave me a bad grade on an essay because of one single word. I could understand him picking apart my spoken Italian on oral exams, but, while I was aware I still had deficiencies as a writer, I found it intolerable that he gave me a bad grade for one mistake, and not keep the big picture in mind. Since I was pretty sure I hadn't spelled anything wrong, I went up to the teacher to complain.

"Why did you circle this in red?" I asked.

"Don't you see the mistake?" he said.

"No."

"Read it out loud."

That particular section of my essay described the first circle of *Inferno*.

"A purplish light shines through the stormy clouds and across a flower-studded field where the great thinkers engage in brilliant conversation."

The smart kids smiled cruelly.

"Flower-studded?" the professor asked.

"Yes."

"Do you know what studded means?"

"Covered with small dots."

The smart kids laughed.

"That's spotted, my dear friend. Something that is studded doesn't have dots or spots or specks; it has studs, which are a kind of support beam or pillar."

The experience embittered me. I didn't care if I made a fool of myself in chemistry, but when I wrote something, I wanted to be praised for it. And, furthermore, this was Dante, an author—should I never achieve any of the grand goals I had set for myself and was forced to fall back on literature—I had chosen as my model. I must improve my vocabulary, I told myself after incidents like that, and most of all, I have to start coming up with uncommonly good literary ideas.

I had one such idea the following year, while reading *Purgatorio*. It revolved around my grandmother, even though our relationship had since changed somewhat. She still doted on me in her annoying way when serving meals, she still worried constantly about my health, she still implemented strategies within our family that allowed me greater comforts than even my father enjoyed. But because, when I turned twelve or thirteen, I had somehow miraculously become older than her, she had started feeling awkward around me. She assumed that I thought everything she said was stupid; she stopped talking to me about her feelings and telling me stories, she boosted her already exaggerated affection for me by believing herself inferior, as if it gave her great pleasure to feel less than nothing in my presence, thereby granting me the right to boss her around and have her do absolutely anything I desired, even killing my father if he made me suffer. One afternoon, while she was stood at the window lost in thought, I went up to her—she was getting shorter every day, while I had grown very tall—and asked, only partially in jest, "Do you love me?"

She had often asked me that question in the past, but I had never put it to her.

"Yes," she replied, worried by my strange behavior.

"Really?"

"Really."

"Then swear to me that, after you die, if something else exists, you'll come and tell me all about it, down to the smallest detail."

All color drained out of her. It must've been too tall of an order for her to fill.

"What if they don't let me?"

We discussed it at length and finally I got her to agree. But it wasn't easy: the saints, the Virgin Mary, Jesus, and God were all real entities to her, she prayed to them with devotion and couldn't tolerate the thought of ruining the special relationship she had with them. By then I was practically an atheist and behind the slightly sarcastic tone of my request was a plan to obtain clarity on the natural and supernatural. If, after dying, my grandmother came back from the dead with rich descriptions of heaven, hell, and purgatory, I'd adapt accordingly, and might even become a monk. However, if she—who, just to make me happy, agreed to even go against God—didn't send me a single message, then I would deduce that nothing existed after death, that all things were destined to repeatedly rise and fall, including the girl from Milan, whom I had practically forgotten by then. Naturally, whether my grandmother came back with heaps of first-hand otherworldly material, or if she remained silent forever and thereby confirmed Nothing, I planned on writing an unforgettable story in which I might even find room for the now-faded specter of the girl from Milan.

### 14.

After I had extracted that promise, amidst giggles and dark thoughts, I put all my religious and funereal concerns aside. I focused instead on my studies, on literary pursuits that regarded other aspects of humanity, and on nocturnal wanderings that did not take into the slightest consideration how my poor grandmother couldn't sleep knowing I wasn't at home and tucked in bed. Then I graduated from high school and set off along the path to university, a mysterious place where none of my relatives had ever set foot, not even by mistake.

I wasted a little time at the beginning because I didn't know which course of study to choose. At first, I enrolled in Engineering to please my father, as he had always wanted me to become a railroad engineer. Then I briefly considered Mathematics because I'd recently met a girl who was studying math, we were going out, and I didn't want to appear less intelligent than her. Finally, I chose the department of

Letters, which seemed like the fastest way to become the greatest writer on the planet.

With this goal in mind, I read night and day, beat-up old volumes purchased for little from street vendors: lots of ancient writers, eighteenth and nineteenth century novellas, novels, and epics, and a fair share of giants of Italian literature, from Guido Cavalcanti to Giacomo Leopardi. I would've gladly read more modern writers but didn't have the money to buy fresh-off-the-press contemporary literature, so I hardly ever ventured into the twentieth century. Even so, I chugged right along. Studying for school had always bored me—all those dates and notes, the homework and grades—but reading for the sake of reading and interrupting it only to urgently dash off my own lyrics, verselets, canticles, canzoni, and decamerons seemed like a pretty good life. Every chance I got, I trained my writing muscles to evoke in future readers thoughts of rebellion against the powerful, empathy for the destitute, an occasional snicker, and, in general, to incite them to dedicate their lives to the benefit of Italy and the world.

But it didn't last. University, even more than school, turned out to be the mortal enemy of reading and writing, and I was forced to accept that I had to take exams, memorize authors' biographies and bibliographies, and be able to regurgitate in proper Italian boring textbooks on history and geography. I ended up wandering up and down hallways, looking for classrooms, trying to understand how to survive amid a crowd of students who were probably just as lost as I was and maybe even shared my overblown ambitions. I knew nothing about the hierarchy of professors, course requirements, how much books and lecture notes cost, class schedules, how to get attendance signatures, or the enormous efforts it took to get basic information from either registrars or building custodians. And so, I proceeded empirically, initially planning to take exams like Latin, Italian, and Greek, which sounded good when lumped together. But these classes were overcrowded and difficult to understand, the books were dull and expensive tomes, and so I fell back on subjects—namely, Papyrology and Glottology—whose chief merit was that their textbooks were slender and not too costly.

There was another reason I chose that route. Papyrology and glottology were words I'd never heard before, definitely not at home but not even at school, and appropriating them seemed like a good way to signal my cultural elegance to friends, relatives and my new girlfriend.

"What exam are you studying for?"

"Papyrology."

"Wow."

"Yeah."

"And then, after that?"

"Glottology."

"Wow."

"Yeah."

Basically, I tried to seem like someone who had a plan for the future. But in actual fact, there was no plan, all I did was dream. One day I felt like I was on the right path, the next day I doubted it entirely. Maybe I wasn't cut out for scholarly work. Maybe I didn't know how to study, recall, or write riveting things. Maybe I'd never know glory and forever be a poorly dressed, disheveled mess, like some oppressed student in Tzarist Russia, toiling to scrounge up enough money to pay for my books by giving lessons to kids only slightly less intelligent than me. In other words, I lived in a constant state of anxiety, as if I were hanging from the top of a glass wall by my fingertips, always on the verge of sliding down into a dark pool of sludge with a horrifying screech. I was careful not to let anyone see this side of me, not even my girlfriend. With everyone, and particularly with her, I employed the constantly bemused tone that I had first adopted around the age of fifteen and that by now I was incapable of altering—some, she more than most, found it entertaining. And yet, not a day went by that I didn't want to slink down some empty street and, without any apparent reason and like never before, howl with despair, kick and punch the air, and cry, if but for a minute. I had even identified the right street—parallel to the train station—and sometimes I walked down it, but I never managed to blow off steam. I just didn't know how.

## 15.

The only person I could be anxious or impatient with, the only person who, despite my ingratitude, continued to reassure me day in and day out, for as long as she lived, thanks to her pure and simple presence in those designated spaces of hers—the kitchen, the sink, the stove, the table, and the window—without ever doubting me or my spectacular destiny, not even for a minute, was, naturally, my grandmother. My enrolling at university made her even more in awe of me while simultaneously allowing her endless opportunities to idolize me. She brought me coffee when I woke up and stood silently by the bed contemplating me while I drank it, waiting for me to hand her back the cup. If she spoke at all, it was to praise me and the miracle that was my every word and gesture. The one time I brought my new girlfriend home for a few minutes, neither my parents nor brothers said a thing, as if my sentimental life was as normal as spring rain. Only she, whom we treated like a piece of furniture and to whom I hadn't even introduced the girl, whispered, Oh, would you look at the two of you, how beautiful.

Only once, after returning home from one of her rare excursions into the world beyond our four walls, was she more expansive, the way she was when I was small. Most days she went out either to buy food or go to the cemetery, where she tended to her husband's burial niche. In both instances, she donned her dark dress—the only formal outfit she owned—as well as proper undergarments, artfully repaired over the years, because she didn't want to die in the street and have people discover her dressed inappropriately. Nothing special happened on those outings and she would return home only a little tired and grumpy. But on this particular occasion, she came back full of vim and vigor, and quickly pulled me aside to tell me how she'd gone to the cemetery to buy my grandfather, in addition to the usual electric votive candle positioned in front of his niche, a wooden *pezzotto* with room for two bulbs so that he could celebrate the holy day of Easter with a little extra light. And then, all of a sudden, the young man in charge of selling lights looked at her and exclaimed: Signora, what a pleasure, do you remember me? It was none other than Lello, my childhood friend. Hello, hello, he kissed her cheeks, gave her a discount, and as she was leaving, he scribbled down his number on a piece of paper and said he really hoped I would call.

My grandmother diligently handed over the piece of paper, but I quickly learned that she had never much liked my friend. Don't call him, she said. In her opinion, Lello had always acted like he was well brought up and spoke in proper Italian, and, sure, the whole building might have thought him good-looking, but compared to me, he was terribly ugly, and what's more he was nasty, he owned a bike and caused me great suffering because I did not.

I had no recollection of having suffered because of Lello's bike and I told her so. Apparently, she suffered in my place without me ever realizing it, but most of all, she didn't like how he cast a shadow over me. Your friend thought he was better than you, but the heavenly father is always fair, and what's your friend now? A big nothing, she said, and this fact filled her with joy. My ugly old friend was working as an electrician at the cemetery while I was studying at university. Don't call him, she insisted, *ènustrúnz*.

I did as she said, but not out of arrogance or to indulge her cruel sense of revenge—even though I couldn't deny that it also felt a little good—but because, right when she said Lello's name, the girl from Milan reappeared before my eyes, after ten long years. The vision lasted only a moment or two: first I saw her on the balcony and then at the fountain. But the amount of detail I saw was incredible. Her mortal life had all but slipped my mind, and yet here she was, back from the dead. I know, I know, the phrase "mortal life" has fallen out of use, and rightly so. The word "mortal" suggests something deadly, like snake venom or those old bottles of poison with the skull and crossbones on them; "mortal" together with "life" makes it sound like life is actually the danger; and most of all, to use the phrase convincingly you need to believe in its opposite, immortal life. But in this day and age, who believes in immortality anymore? With the gradual waning of that notion, the pairing of "mortal life" has also faded, with the adjective "mortal" now seeming to most people—me included—as sinister or merely redundant. But back then—what was it, 1962?—recalling the girl and her mortal life seemed normal and—for no reason at all, like when you shiver after feeling a warm breeze—the girl from Milan came to life.

I managed to keep her in my thoughts for an hour, a day, maybe even two, but she wouldn't settle. I'd look at girls out on the street, girls around the age of eighteen, and think to myself: if she had lived, if she had grown up normally, would she now look like that? But the image only lasted a few seconds because those real bodies, full of throbbing life, chased hers away; her wick was too short. I remember something similar happening one night while I was trying to fall asleep. I saw her and her alone, independent of any other female image, either real or invented. She sat on the side of my bed, a rough sketch of a girl-woman, and spoke to me in a language that I couldn't understand. It might've been English, but she pronounced it well, not like the anglo-italo-neapolitan that I spoke and worked hard to correct. I listened with utmost care and attention, didn't understand a thing, and then lost her in my sleep.

Essentially, she came back to me the same way you perceive a road signal: you're driving along when you see a triangular sign, it sends a sudden alert to your brain that there will be a sharp turn, animals on the road, or a railroad crossing with no gates, so you proceed with caution for a bit, and then you forget all about it and erase it from your mind. I'd be lying if I said I threw away Lello's phone number so the girl from Milan would return to the dead. I think I did it for a more general reason. I probably realized that if I did call him, I wouldn't know what to say beyond the usual "when we were kids" stuff. At the age of nineteen, I still had no desire to reminisce about my childhood. Just thinking about it made me feel embarrassed, as did my adolescence for that matter. I felt certain that I had been clumsy and ridiculous during both those phases of life; there was little to recall that was either moving or sweet. To tell the truth, I wish I had come into this world around the age of seventeen, thereby sparing me all the stupidities of the first sixteen.

## 16.

The truth is, even the years between the ages of sixteen and eighteen were rocky ones. I was always on the brink of regressing and constantly needed support to quell my fears. My grandmother worked just fine, all told. Her manner of hanging on my every word and watching me closely was like cod liver oil: it tasted awful but was fortifying. Each time I left the house, she'd timidly ask me three questions.

"Where are you going?"

"To the university," I replied, annoyed that she had asked.

"Coming back for lunch?"

"No, I'll be back later, tonight, not sure when," I said, even more annoyed than before.

And then came the third and most reverential question, almost a whisper.

"What are you going to study?"

"Papyrology," I said, and she looked at me in amazement.

Thus fortified, I walked out, skipped down the stairs, made my way through the crowd in Piazza Garibaldi, strode with confidence down the Rettifilo all the way to the university, and into my Papyrology class.

Even though there weren't many students in the class, the professor never addressed us directly. I only recall seeing him from the back, keenly communicating his science to the large, rectangular chalkboard in front of him, writing down, in white on black, details about the papyrus scrolls at Herculaneum.

The lessons were no doubt excellent, but I got distracted easily. One morning while he was explaining just how difficult it was to unroll those archaeological finds, I started reflecting on the dangers of Vesuvius and eruptions in general, about words like *putizze*, the foul smelling emanations of hydrogen sulfide, and *mofette*, other gaseous discharges, as well as pyroclastic flows; I thought about those pastel-colored, vine-adorned images of the volcano that show it starting to spew hellfire and death in the middle of a dance of satyrs bloated with local wine, then smothering, burning, decimating entire cities, together with their pretentious politics, and all their strange living creatures, who either screamed or whispered their final words, while by chance, purely by chance, only the words written on charred papyruses and protected by lava stone—the silent words of an Epicurean who had died long before, the excellent Philodemus of Gadara, with his mortuary characters carved into another death, that of the green marshy reeds used to make Egyptian paper—remained; despite all the burning and charring, they waited for centuries to be read again, to be spoken aloud, a voice for today, tomorrow, and forever.

It was in one of those moments of distraction that the girl from Milan came back in full force and tried to dig herself a more stable spot in my life. I can't say exactly how it happened. Maybe it was the image of Vesuvius, the great destroyer; maybe it was the notion that people on our planet are endlessly dying, that individuals and masses are constantly being wiped out, and this thought was so devastating that even the gods regretted letting it happen; maybe it was simply that my head was full of literary ideas and I was looking for a way to use them. The fact is that the girl from Milan broke through with even greater force than she had at the sound of Lello's name. And since my girlfriend was waiting for me after class, I didn't hold back, and I told her that tale of misfortune and grief.

I told her everything, surprising myself by how much I remembered: how she danced on the parapet, the rain, the white petals, the duel, my delirium. And in the passionate Italian that we spoke together, I came to the perhaps excessive conclusion that although practically everything having to do with the girl from Milan was gone, while listening to the professor lecture, I realized that the girl and her voice existed inside my head like some charred papyrus that a machine—some eighteenth-century contraption—was delicately unrolling, restoring to me the story of my tumultuous first love.

The name of my analytically-minded girlfriend was Nina, and she had a sweet and lively gaze. She listened to me without ever interrupting, and surely with not a little surprise. Up until then, she knew me to be an amusing young man and had fallen in love with me, I believe, for my sense of irony, for how I always managed to be lighthearted about things. However, after this long speech she must have realized just how unhinged I really was, practically another person entirely, someone capable of combining Vesuvius, Pompei, Herculaneum, and a girl from Milan, thereby creating my own personal, lower-middle class apocalypse.

"What a horrible experience," she said with a shudder when the story ended.

"Yes."

"How old were you?"

"Nine."

"What about her?"

"Eight."

"Oh, you poor darling."

"Yeah, but it was a long time ago."

"Even so, it left its mark on you."

"Not too deep, just a little. I was a kid."

Our verbal exchanges were more or less of this tenor: affectionate and courteous. We were trying to become, with each passing day, a cultured couple capable of blending eros, papyrology, glottology, and a pinch—but just a small one—of algebra. Nina came from my same background, no one from her family had ever gone beyond elementary school. Consequently, and with a little exaggeration on my part, we sought to craft our own reflective, bookish way of being together out of nothing. Our interests ran the gamut: we talked about books, film, and theater. Every so often we dabbled in subjects like class warfare, American imperialism, racism, decolonization, and the destruction of humankind in the impending atomic war. But we still had a lot to learn about those subjects. I knew less about them than I did about papyrology and glottology, and this was probably true for Nina, too. We felt more at ease when we discussed our feelings and the problems of being in a relationship.

Around the time I told her about the girl from Milan, the subject that we talked about most frequently was fidelity. She leaned towards absolute faithfulness.

"One thing I can't accept is cheating," she said once, her gentle manner cracking ever so slightly.

"I care less about monogamy than honesty," I replied.

"Which is to say?"

"If I like another girl, I'll tell you."

"Before or after you cheat on me?"

"Before. Otherwise, where's the honesty?"

"I don't agree with you on this."

"Would you rather I tell you after?"

"No. You have to want me, and only me, forever. If you can't, it's better if we break up now."

Sooner or later even those conversations reached a limit we didn't know how to get beyond, so we'd drop it, and go back, if anything, to talking about the girl from Milan. Actually, it was Nina who periodically asked me questions about the traumatic event, either because she was genuinely curious, or just to humor me. I liked it. I gradually realized that the more I talked about the girl, the more she came back to life.

"Did she always play on her own?" Nina asked once.

"Yes," I said.

"She danced?"

"Yes."

"On the ledge?"

"Yes."

"Was she good?"

"Yes."

Just then, at that point in our conversation, things suddenly grew very complex, and in an altogether unexpected way. To justify the weight I gave the story, I told Nina with some exaggeration that I considered the girl from Milan to be the mold on which all my future girlfriends were based, that she was a kind of prototype without which I might never have realized that I was in love with Nina herself.

After listening carefully, Nina commented softly. "You just said something that frightens me."

"What did I say?"

"You just put me on the same plane as the dead girl."

"To show you how much I love you."

"Fine, but it's still shocking. The girl died in a fire?"

"No, she drowned."

"So, what's the connection between Herculaneum and the papyri again?"

"The human condition, destruction, memory."

"You know, I really don't like being associated with such a dark memory."

"Literature is full of situations like that."

"So are the lives of unhappy couples."

This last comment sounded to me like an alarm, so I promised myself to talk less about the subject in the future. I valued being that lovable and charming man who knew how to kindle lightness. So, I did something silly, like jumping in the air and clicking my heels together—which she adored—and let her accompany me to Glottology.

## 17.

We had our routines by then. I used to pick her up at Mathematics, she'd wait for me at Papyrology, and she often accompanied me to the Cortile del Salvatore, where

Glottology was held. Back then it felt like I loved her more than any of my classes, so I was almost always late to my next class because I wanted to spend as much time as possible with her.

Glottology wasn't crowded but nor was it entirely deserted. If I was late, I had to sit in the last row. Generally speaking, if you sit in the last row or the first one, it doesn't make a lot of difference, but this professor—who was around fifty, and therefore in the prime of life—spoke in such a soft voice it was as if he had decided to teach only the people sitting in the front row. He leaned towards his most faithful followers and trilled delicately but indistinctly, sharing his rich linguistic and etymological knowledge, ignoring those of us who arrived late. In fact, after straining our ears for the first ten minutes, we always gave up and spent the remainder of the class getting to know each other, sharing phone numbers and addresses, and organizing dance parties.

I managed to overhear something only on the rare occasions when I obtained a seat in the second or third row, which was when I discovered that the professor was especially interested in the toponyms of the regions of Abruzzo and Molise, in particular those formed by two nouns or by a noun and adjective, such as Monteleone or Campobasso. But I also learned that language is in constant flux, that voices sound and resound in many more ways than the twenty-six letters of the alphabet can communicate, and that there was a constantly growing need to invent more letters; for example, there was a strange -z, a thin capital -s, and a backwards -e.

Even more than in Papyrology, I only needed to hear a few comments and off I'd go on a tangent, as they say.

The proof lies in my notebooks from that first year, chock full of frenzied notes. Abruzzo and Molise—places I had never seen—became detailed landscapes of smooth or craggy or jagged rock faces, filled in the springtime with huge swathes of green leaves and flowers, and striated with dark or yellowing bare branches in the winter, always slashed through by strips of grey-blue falling water that went on to flow between the mountains, across the valley floor, occasionally getting lost in flat bogs or dark grottoes, but for the most part becoming gurgling, rolling, foaming streams, dappled by the variegated songs of birds and the hum of voices rising from human settlements that huddled here and there in warm and sunny spots, either on a mountain or in a valley or in a clearing near the ravines or by cascading brooks and rivers, by ditches, canals, willow trees (whose branches were used to make baskets), and pools and dams and weirs, by brush and scrub, the *sterpo* and its metathesis *streppo*, so that when humans encountered each other, they started saying I live in the valley, I live on the mountain, I live by the river, and so on, from one generation to the next, they and their descendants going on to live in places that were named after geographical formations: Vallocchia della Grottolicchia, Solagna della Foia, Stroppara di Fosso Vrecciato, the very same way that we lived in Naples, Nea Polis, the new city, and how we marched down the Rettifilo, a taut line, or sat around bored at Mezzocannone, which to my mind meant half, a wartime weapon that shot half-sized cannonballs.

But I have to admit that I was more interested in language generally, in the way sounds are formed by windy tempests inside oral cavities, in the way sound waves broke into infinitesimal fragments against the teeth, in the way most of the flowers of the voice blossom in the air only to wither without ever getting transcribed, while others find a place within the alphabet, and yet are short-lived and never entirely stable: one scribble chases away its predecessor merely because the scribe was Emilian or Calabrian or Neapolitan and pronounced things differently than the Tuscan or Ligurian, so, for example, *etterno* became *eterno*, *sanza* became *senza*, *schera* took on an -i and transformed into *schiera*; with the abandoned forms falling tragically into nothingness, and all this taking place back when it seemed that the sun would never set on pen and paper, when erudite people confidently and clear-headedly wrote out *etterno* with beating heart, by candlelight, and then— just like that—one -t is gone, considered superfluous, to the extent that if today you write *etterno*, somebody will circle it in red: spelling mistake.

I also learned how phonemes are classified, and discovered that -a -e -i -o -u was really nothing more than a children's song, and that, actually, vowels are much more complex: there are the basic ones (-i, -a, -u) and there are the middle ones (-e and -o) and that the combinations of -i and -a or -a and -u are, in theory, infinite. When writing the letter -i, what specific vibration was I referring to? Where exactly does my tongue go? And when they get written out, aren't those signs (-i, -a, -u) inherently flawed and deficient? Don't they leave out, precisely because of their inadequacies, imperceptible phonic alloys and all the colored filaments of voice? While the professor lectured, I saw silvery layers of sound—I'm still copying from my old notes here—get chiseled away by the movements of the tongue in the mouth, I saw articulations and explosive bursts of breath more colorful than those illustrated by Rimbaud in his sonnet about vowels. And then I discovered that all those alloys, all those long-ignored colors could be captured with phonetic symbols. That alphabet came as a true revelation to me, and when the professor wrote out some of the symbols on the chalkboard, I felt a surge of optimism: ð ɯ ɵ ŋ ʕ ʮ ɸ ʂ ç ɹ j. I couldn't wait to master them and figure out how to adapt them to my literary goals, and even invent new ones, if needed.

Back then I used to get excited easily. I'd start to sweat, and blood pounded through my veins. The next time I saw Nina after one of those classes, I wrote down: ę ẹ ö ü ɛ ɑ ɔ ʉ. She replied with a look that said: ?

## 18.

Everything I learned, I summarized for her. I recapped the lessons, or even declaimed my notes to her, either way she listened in rapture. I now think she may well have been pretending. I have since come to terms with the fact that even people who love us often have a hard time holding themselves back to leave room for our incessant need to be the center of attention. Back then, though, I was certain that Nina was thrilled to be inundated with my idiocies. I was confident I had found someone who believed in my exceptional nature even more than my grandmother, and definitely more than me.

The truth of the matter was naturally far more complex. When one of Nina's classes ended, she walked out with a head full of formulas, and probably would've liked to talk about algebra the same way I did about papyrology and glottology. But since she knew that I understood nothing about algebra, as well as many other things, she behaved politely, as if a strand of barbed wire had been extended between the mathematical calculations that took place in her head and my world, comprised of Philodemus of Gadara, the toponyms of Abruzzo and Molise, my convoluted discussions about vowels, and the squiggles of phonetic writing. Or, even more probable—given this was 1962-63—she assumed that it was her role as a woman to pay close attention to what I, as a man, learned, to encourage me in my pursuit of an education in the humanities, to be amused by and laugh at my humorous comments and smallest sighs, and to look at me in awe when I made deeply profound observations.

And yet, even back then, it was never a good idea to go too far. While some of my comments were warmly welcomed, others, and with increasing frequency, brought out a fighting spirit hidden deep inside that gentle girl.

I took increasing pleasure in showing her how everything was destined to crumble, especially things that had once seemed lasting and that I loved. Once, I walked out of Glottology in a bad mood.

"Language isn't static! Language disintegrates, along with writing," I declared as if some new danger threatened us.

"So do mountains, planets, and stars. So does the entire universe," she said.

"But, for me, writing is something I rely on. Discovering that it's fragile and insubstantial is disorienting."

"What do you mean?"

"The alphabet doesn't cover all the sounds we make, Nina. You have no idea how much gets left out."

"I guess that's just something you're just going to have to learn to accept."

"It's not that easy. It's like the girl from Milan. I remember so few of her words and yet I continue to hear them in some part of my brain. And inside that echo, the vowel sounds I hear don't line up with the five letters we have. I'm scared that if I try and write out the few sentences she said to me with letters from the alphabet, that little bit of voice I hear in my memory will definitively die, just like she has."

She countered me with an unhappy silence.

"Again with the drowned girl?" she eventually asked.

"It was just an example."

"I'm a little tired of hearing about the eruptions of Vesuvius, the way language is crumbling, how words can't keep up with voices and sounds, and how everything is decaying and perishing."

"Don't you love me anymore?"

She thought about it for a second. "No, I still do. But come over to this side, forget about the dead girl from Milan, and while I'm still alive, think about me."

I realized that in order to make that statement she had momentarily stepped back from the two of us, observed me from a distance, and discovered that she didn't much like the way I kept making room for the shadow of the girl. She wanted me to be the person I had led her to believe I was, someone amusing, never pretentious, not even when discussing ambitions, capable of bringing light to the inevitably dark corners of life. As a matter of fact, afterward she started asking me things like, what's going on? Are you tired? Are you having some kind of nervous breakdown? Should we talk about it? She was sweet but anxious, and I had a hard time convincing her that I was fine and that only idiots were consistently happy. Sure, it was true, at times I felt like death was all around but—I reassured her—I just had to forget the girl from Milan and it would all pass. In this we were helped by a far different set of worries. Nina told me that her period was late. She was scared and consequently I was too. I couldn't sleep at night, I imagined myself a father, I'd have to stop studying, cut short all my literary ambitions, find some kind of job, and provide for my family. We spent a lot of time imagining—while tragically listening to Albinoni's *Adagio*—a hurried wedding, her pregnancy, the birth. But she, luckily, continued with the scalding hot baths. It seemed pointless, at first, but then she was cured, which is to say she got her period.

We considered it a miracle, it felt marvelous to be alive, and we went back to being students in love. But then, one morning, and to my great surprise, she brought up the dead girl, and she did it with sarcasm.

"Can I ask you something?"

"Sure."

"Why do you always call her the girl from Milan?"

"Because she was a girl who came from Milan."

"But she had a name, right?"

The question was unsettling. I had never really thought about it. What was her name? How was it possible that I didn't know the name of the girl from Milan? How was it that I knew the name of Philodemus, that he came from Gadara, when he was born, when he died, and that he was an Epicurean, but I had no idea of the girl's first name, and moreover it had taken me ten years since her death to realize it?

"Of course she had a name," I admitted. "But I never knew it."

"Do you know mine?"

"Yes."

"What is it?"

"Nina."

And with that, she walked off—maybe happy, maybe not—to her algebra class.

19.

I went home more displeased with myself than usual. Realizing that the girl from Milan had not only lost her life but also her name made the pillars holding up the universe, and even punctuation, crumble. I felt like an Adam who, while aspiring to build a lasting language, forgets to name one essential thing, leaving a dropped stitch in the woven fabric of language, a flaw that will gradually lead to its dissolution.

I wandered around the empty apartment—my brothers were at school, my father at work, my mother out delivering the clothes she tailored for her affluent clients—forcing myself to accept the hypothesis that although I wasn't guilty, objectively speaking, for the early end of the girl's mortal life, I was guilty of not being able to say: this was her name, these were her words, and thereby allow her to endure.

I peered into the kitchen in search of company, knowing I would find my grandmother there. She was ably chopping parsley with a knife.

"What was grandfather's name?" I asked casually.

"Giuseppe."

"Yes, I know that, but what did you call him?"

"Giuseppe."

"I mean between the two of you, in private. Didn't you ever use another name?"

"Peppe."

"What else?"

"Pe'."

"And which of those was his real name, the one you could call out right now, and he would appear, even though he died all those years ago?"

She looked at me strangely, probably scared I was teasing her. But seeing that I was serious, instead she muttered, *nunniàsturià?* She wanted me to make good use of my time, not waste it on her; studying was much more important than all this chitchat about Nonno's name. But I continued to ask her about the names and nicknames they used for each other—the ones they used when they joked around, when they held each other tight—at which point she started laughing uncontrollably, a warm, gaptoothed chuckle. She replied by saying that names were for people who were alive, when you called out to the dead they never answered, her husband had never answered her even though she had called him lots of times. And it wasn't because he was unkind. When he was alive, he always answered her when he could. He had even answered her the morning he fell off the building. Before getting out of bed to prepare his lunch tin, she had said his name, Pe', in a whisper, and even though he was still sleepy, he turned to her and hugged her and kissed her. Kissed her, she repeated with a giggle, and she kept talking with growing amusement, which was rare for her, about what she called "the sweet stuff of life." She told me that if my girlfriend ever called my name, I should never say not now, I'm busy, maybe later, because for her, later was always wrong. Better immediately, that very instant. And then suddenly she recalled the promise I had forced her to make when I was younger—to come back after she died and tell me what existed on the other side. Well, she'd given it some thought and there was no need to wait until she died, she could tell me right there and then, it had all become clear to her while she was chopping parsley. At that point, her laughter grew hysterical, her face turned bright red, her eyes shone brightly, and she couldn't stop. She had realized that there was nothing after death: no God, no Virgin Mary, no saints, no hell, no purgatory, nothing. She pointed to the parsley on the chopping board, the fragments edged with their greenish liquid. This—she said—this is what comes after. She would become like that parsley, and she didn't mind, no, actually it made her feel lighter, that's what she would become: chopped parsley. And that's why, she insisted, I should go call Nina right now, she's such a pretty girl. Go on, call her, hold each other tight, *ahcommebèll.*

### 20.

I called Nina and cleared the air somewhat. To be honest, she wasn't that sweet with me anymore; her devotion had faded and she often behaved like a Deanira, less keen on washing Heracles' tunics than dirtying them intentionally. At the same time, it felt like our relationship, now past the initial phase of dissembling in order to please each other, had taken on a solid and positive predictability. We went back to dividing our time between papyrology, glottology, and love spats.

One day, while strolling around Piazza Municipio—we had gone to visit the Biblioteca Nazionale, where neither of us had ever been—I heard someone shout, Mimí! I turned around even though no one had called me that in a very long time, not even my grandmother. A dilapidated, white Fiat 600 came up alongside us, driven by a young man with slicked back blond hair, a wide forehead, blue eyes, and a dazzling smile. Mimí, the guy said again, it's me, Lello, don't you recognize me?

I recognized him. Or rather, I recognized the child flailing around in the driver's wide face, which resembled that of a Norwegian sailor. It really was Lello, and before I knew it, he had pulled over and jumped out of the car, arms open wide. He was so deeply moved that even I ended up getting emotional. I hugged him back, noticing how unfamiliar his broad shoulders, strong chest, and deep voice were, and realizing my only assurance that it was truly him was that oscillating, flame-like presence of the child that flickered before my eyes, bending, practically vanishing, and then returning.

I introduced him to Nina, but he was so excited about bumping into me that he didn't pay much attention to her. Instead, he started inundating me with questions: how were my brothers, my parents, my grandmother?

"I saw her once," he said, "she was so sweet. I asked her to give you my phone number, I was hoping you'd call."

I lied. "She must've forgotten, but hey, we're here now. How lucky."

"What're you up to these days, Mimí?"

"I go to the university."

"What are you studying?"

"Ancient languages. What about you?"

"Aeronautical engineering."

"Ah."

"I knew you'd study something like ancient languages."

"Yeah, nothing modern. The ancients always seemed much more reliable."

"Where are you living these days?"

"We live in a Ferrovia building not far from the station."

"We moved about a year after you did."

"And where are you living now?"

"Not far from here, on Via Verdi. Hey, do you want to come up? I can make you two a coffee."

"No, thank you," I said, replying for Nina.

He didn't want to let us go. "How about we go for a drive? What do you think?"

"Some other time, sure."

"Oh sorry, I didn't mean to interrupt something."

"You're not, not at all!"

"Yes, I am. Hey, look, why don't you guys take my car and go for a drive? I'll give you the keys, then you can park it on Via Verdi, and come upstairs for a bit afterwards."

"Thanks, but I don't have a license."

"You haven't gotten your driver's license yet?"

"No."

"You have to get one!"

"I know, I know. But it's so expensive. As soon as I save up some money, I'll sign up for classes."

At that point Nina interrupted the conversation. She was apparently tired of being ignored.

"I study Mathematics," she offered politely.

"Wow, I never would've guessed."

"Why?"

"No, just because."

"No, I'm curious. Why did you say that?"

"Because girls who study math are usually as ugly as sin."

"Same with guys who study engineering."

"True, true."

"Actually, I wouldn't mind going for a drive."

"Where to?"

Nina thought for a minute. "The place where you two played when you were kids."

Both Lello and I were happy with that proposal. He got behind the wheel, my girlfriend climbed into the back, and I sat in front because I had long legs and would've been uncomfortable in the back seat. As we headed up towards Vomero, I praised Lello for the skill and ease with which he risked our lives while darting through traffic.

"Tell me about the girl you both used to watch. What was she like?" Nina said.

"What girl?" Lello asked.

"The girl from Milan," I said, expecting him to remember.

Lello squinted as if peering off into the distance, far beyond the windshield, but saw nothing. "I don't remember a girl from Milan."

Nina refreshed his memory. "The one you dueled over."

"I remember our duels!"

"But then she went on vacation and died . . . " she offered.

"Oh yeah, I remember something."

"What exactly do you remember?" I asked.

"I remember you wrote really scary stories about horrifying ghosts. And how obsessed you were that there was a pit full of the dead in the courtyard."

"What? A pit?" Nina looked at me as if I had hidden an important detail.

"It's nothing," I said with embarrassment, but Lello went on.

"When Mimí was a kid, he always used to talk about dead people, dangerous chases, killings. He had a wild imagination." He paused for a second and then looked over at me as if he had had a brilliant idea. "Hey, do you want to come work with me at the cemetery?"

I pretended to be surprised. "You work at the cemetery?"

"Yeah, they hire university students to sell lighting contracts for the tombs and burial niches."

"Sounds like the perfect job for Mimí."

"It does, doesn't it?" Lello said, trying to encourage me. "Just think of all the terrifying ideas for stories you'd get. And at the same time, you could earn a little money for your driver's license."

I shook my head. "Thanks, that's nice of you, but I already do too much tutoring."

We parked the car and—with Nina in the center, me to her right, and Lello to her left—we walked around the piazza where, around ten years earlier, he'd run me over with his bike. I reminded him of it, hoping he'd remember at least that.

"Luckily nothing serious happened," he said apologetically as if it had just happened.

"Nothing serious? You tore up my whole foot and ankle, all the way up to my knee. Blood came gushing out."

"Really? I only remember a few scratches."

"Don't pay attention to him," Nina offered. "He has a tendency to exaggerate."

"It bled a lot," I insisted. "I had to go wash it off at the fountain."

I looked over, the fountain was still there, a witness that spoke no words, only gurgled. I left Lello and Nina for a minute and went to drink, curious to discover if I'd hear the words of the girl again, and I did. For a few, intense seconds I heard all the tonalities in her voice. But I didn't say anything to Lello when I got back. His bad memory risked weakening my own.

He was the one who wanted to show Nina where the pit was. We walked into the courtyard but couldn't find it. Recent construction had modified the space and impoverished our youth. Both Lello and I were disappointed.

"Do you remember that loud thudding we heard all of a sudden?" he asked.

"Yes."

"It was probably just a water pump."

I hesitated, and then grinned a little. "It was the dead."

"Oh, would you just shut up with your invented dead people," Nina said with exasperation. "He works at a cemetery and definitely knows more than you do about stuff like that."

But Lello defended me and praised my narrative skills, saying that no one told stories about the dead the way I did, which, although he said it seriously, amused my girlfriend to no end. I let them get acquainted and have a little fun at my expense while surreptitiously leading them to the area below the girl's balcony. I couldn't help it, it was my first experience with death, after all. Everything seemed so much dingier, as if the sky and buildings had once been painted on the canopy of an open umbrella, but now the structure was broken, and the umbrella was closing in on the person underneath it.

"Now do you remember the girl from Milan?" I asked Lello.

He looked at the run-down façade and its balconies.

"Yeah, a little."

"That was her balcony, up there, on the third floor. Remember?"

"Yeah, a little."

I pointed out my old windows to Nina, and the ledge that connected the bathroom to the kitchen that I had made my way across a couple of times, risking my life. Lello suddenly got very excited.

"The one thing I'll never forget is when you brought down your grandfather's walking stick with the sword inside."

I studied him closely to see if he was joking and didn't say anything for a few seconds. He seemed to be relishing the memory of the lie.

"Your grandfather carried a walking stick with a sword inside?" Nina asked.

"Yes," Lello replied on my behalf. "It had a silver handle and a very sharp sword inside."

"When we were dueling, did you see the girl dancing on the ledge?" I asked him.

Lello thought about it for a minute and then exclaimed, "Yes! I did! That's exactly what happened. And then you stabbed me in the arm with your grandfather's sword."

It was a fantastic moment. We had both gotten caught in the thick tangle of childhood memories, and yet neither of us felt embarrassed about it, and consequently I suddenly felt a deep bond of friendship for him that I'd never felt as a child. I confirmed his version of the event moment by moment.

"You could've killed him," Nina said.

"Yeah."

"Can't leave you men alone for a minute. You're all crazy."

"Yeah."

Overall, revisiting those places and events was a pleasant experience. We walked back to the Fiat 600 happy, and not just Lello and me, but Nina, too. Although she'd grown up in a completely different part of Naples, she now felt so comfortable in our childhood that, once we returned to the car, she gestured that I should squeeze into the back, she sat down in the passenger seat next to Lello, and off we went.

Our driver proved to be even more reckless on the return than on the way there. He drove well, and although he constantly put our lives at risk, he did it so casually that we were able to relax and enjoy the ride. Even when he passed a car on a curve, it was as if there was no chance we'd ever crash into an oncoming bus and die.

Before leaving us in Piazza Municipio, Lello repeated his invitation to come work with him at the cemetery. He was there on Sundays and Mondays from eight in the morning until one in the afternoon. He earned two thousand lire a day for writing up contracts and collecting payments, and two thousand lire a day for electrical work.

"Think it over," he said. "Write down my number."

I jotted down his number, and he took down mine as well as Nina's, who, while we were saying that we should do something together again soon, turned to him and asked, "What was the girl's name?"

Lello pretended to struggle to remember, but by then it was amply clear that the girl from Milan had not had as much of an impact on him as she had had on me.

"It's on the tip of my tongue, but I just can't remember,"

he said, shaking his head. Then he got back in the car and drove off.

Nina and I went back to strolling down the street, arms around each other. A gentle breeze blew in from the sea that smelled good.

"Clearly, you were loads of fun when you were a kid," she said ironically. "What a happy childhood, with all those dead people and killings."

"Actually, I was a lot of fun. Lello doesn't remember anything. What did you think of him?"

"He seems a little dumb, actually."

"I don't know about dumb, but he never had much imagination."

"Well, he obviously cares a lot about you. Not only was he willing to lend us his car, he even offered you a job. You could've been a little nicer with him."

"I have lots of studying and writing to do. The last thing I need now is to try and sell lights to dead people," I said.

Ending in that way was not a good idea. Briefly, my old anxiety came rushing back and I found myself thinking: actually, it really must be very dark down there.

21.

Things with Lello worked out nicely. A few days later, he reached out and invited us to go with him on a day trip to Pompei. We accepted because Nina had never seen the ruins and I, while now quite knowledgeable about the papyri of Herculaneum, had only been there once, when I was eleven and with my parents.

We had a good time together; he was polite, never invasive, and refused all contributions toward gas money. After that first trip, we took others, traveling up and down the Amalfi coast, even down to Pozzuoli, where we saw the Solfatara for the first time. As a result of spending time together, our friendship grew, with Lello even inviting us to the cemetery to see where he worked. It wasn't that bad. He introduced us to his colleagues, all of whom were university students and very polite. Each one had their own office, which was nothing more than a table and chair inside a chapel where they received their clients, which is to say the relatives of the deceased.

Lello was eager to show us his spot. It was tidy, quiet, there was even an altar, crucifix, and votive candles. You could hear birds chirping, the soft sound of leaves fluttering, water gurgling from the fountains, there was the smell of fresh flowers and wilted ones, and that's it: no shouting, no car horns. He kept his personal items—his register, a few pens, textbooks he studied during break, and even a snack—in an empty burial niche, the stone cover off to one side.

We even got to see him at work, and he was good at it, full of sympathy. He mostly sold *pezzotti*, rectangular pieces of wood with either two or four electric votives in them, but sometimes eight (each lit votive cost 100 lire a day), which relatives purchased for their loved ones on special holidays, boosting the standard eternal flame. But his job also entailed—as soon as he saw some devoted widow deep in prayer—getting people to pay up what they owed (the eternal flame cost 465 lire per month). In the role of debt collector, Lello was perfect. First he asked about the deceased, making small talk about what kind of person they had been and only then, after a little chit-chat, got to the question of money, but he made it sound like he was saying: if you really don't have the money, I can pay for you out of my own pocket, but then, if you can't settle your accounts, I'll be forced to switch off the eternal flame. We saw such a scene take place, and in the end the widow paid up everything she owed while mumbling woefully: *però nun me date 'o schiant 'e truvà a mariteme stutàto*, words that expressed how, if the light got switched off (*stutàto*) because of late payments, for her it would be as though her deceased husband was getting switched off (*si stutàsse*) for a second time.

There and then I'm not entirely sure I liked the experience much. Lello's cemetery seemed remote from my idea of what a cemetery should be. Basically, he had made it into his own personal villa with a well-maintained garden, no ghosts, no angels with black feathers, none of the jaundiced despair of death. Even grief became routine. Lello received mourning relatives as if they were guests, as though the lighting—thanks to which the deceased didn't have to rest in malodorous, dark places but in clean, well-lit ones—was his gift to them. Me, I tended to see cemeteries pretty much everywhere, even at parties, or when a friend came up to me and said, "Hey, look alive," I'd have to stop and ask myself, what did he mean by that? Look alive? Am I really dead? In any case, because I didn't want to upset Nina—who liked it there, she started joking around with Lello, saying she almost envied him, how much easier it must be to concentrate there than at home or at the department, she even said she'd be interested in taking the job he had offered me—in order not upset her, I said something along the lines of: bravo, Lello, this is great training, if you can live and work in a cemetery, you can live and work anywhere. Naturally I wasn't as convincing then as I am today, and my awkwardness must have been apparent, because he looked at me strangely.

"What do you mean?" he asked.

"I mean that a person has to get used to the idea that we live among mortal remains."

"I don't get it."

I tried to explain. "We spend half of our life studying the mortal remains of others and the other half creating mortal remains of our own."

Lello had no idea if I was joking or serious, and to tell the truth, neither did I.

"So, you're saying that all of history, geography, physics, chemistry, novels, poetry, algebra, and aeronautical engineering are just mortal remains?"

"Yes."

Nina burst out laughing and looked at Lello. "See what kind of guy your buddy is?"


## 22.

Unquestionably, our rekindled friendship benefitted me. The girl from Milan managed to definitively find firm footing and her new life settled into a revitalized backdrop, rich in details. I didn't risk writing about her, though. I still didn't feel like I had the right tools. But one day, in glottology class, I discovered that the professor thought that transcribing a famous prose passage into phonetic writing was an excellent exercise. It could be a short story or a page from *Promessi sposi* or one from *I Malavoglia*. I recall a few lines from a well-known fable: "*I due litiganti kom'vennero allo:ra ke ssarεbbe ritenu:to pju ffɔrte ki ffosse riuʃʃi:to a ffar si ke il viaddʒato:re si toʎʎesse il mantεllo di dɔsso.*" That exercise proved to me that even the most elegant writing profited from being enriched with phonetic symbols, and so I practiced often and eagerly. I planned on becoming an expert in the language and using it to write an avant-garde story about the girl from Milan, based on my memory of her unparalleled Italian.

Meanwhile, however, the time was fast approaching when I would have to buckle down and study, which is to say memorize long passages in textbook Italian by reciting them out loud. I wanted to begin my university career with the glottology exam, and then immediately after, I'd take papyrology. But when I went to buy the books and lecture notes at the Libreria Scientifica, I learned that the professor's whispering and mumbling had deprived me of one important bit of information: not only was the exam based on the toponyms of Abruzzo and Molise, but we also had to fill out five hundred index cards in phonetic writing, each one dedicated to a different word in Neapolitan dialect.

I went home and shut myself in my room, I stopped seeing Lello and even Nina for a while and resigned myself to hard labor. I realized that the task meant collecting linguistic material in the very moment it was being spoken. I realized that, first and foremost, I'd have to put aside my own way of hearing in order to transcribe other people's speech without bias. I realized I'd have to go out into the fields and talk to people who were busy tilling, find a way to get into the farmer's shed and the old witch doctor's hovel, weasel my way into the mountain hermit's hut and artisan's workshop, and extract words from the mouths of random people—more or less resistant to any form of intellectual discipline—whom I encountered on my wanderings as an aspiring glottologist. I realized that the job entailed finding out if the speakers had ever left their native villages, if they had only and always spoken in dialect, if they had all their teeth and perfect hearing. I realized that my own ears needed to be free of obstruction so that I could detect all the consonant sounds uttered by my interlocutors, especially split and doubled consonants, as well as the entire range of open or closed vowel sounds. I realized that I'd have to invent subtle tricks to get people to talk, people who were naturally shy, sometimes simple, often mistrusting, and occasionally nasty. I realized that I'd have to repress the air of books that surrounded me, hide my papers and pen, and win over the trust of people who were unreasonably suspicious of having their words "etternalized." Finally, I realized that to prepare for this task, I would have to draw on my own knowledge of dialect, show that I could sidle up to unsuspecting folk, and prove I had acquired a high level of competency in transcribing the phonetics of Neapolitan. My task, if I wanted to pass the glottology examination, was to fill out those five hundred index cards as best as I could.

I don't want to exaggerate because eventually I grew to love the very questions and problems I mention above. But, on first impact, I have to confess that it felt like the exam was a debasing of the university, academia in general, and phonetic writing in particular. I thought I had been rising toward an oral and written Italian that was far more elegant than the one used in secondary school, and I had even started formulating promising notions about the complex relationship between speech and sign. Instead, to get my university degree, I was forced to lower myself, and ask the highly uneducated—which is to say people who spoke a dialect that hadn't been corrupted by Italian—the word in Neapolitan for, let's say, the hoop that goes around a wine barrel, a cow's teat, the verb used for draining pus out of a boil, or what a person would say to a loose woman, exposing myself to the risk that my informers, struggling to make ends meet despite their advanced age, would say, get lost, *guagliónummerómperocàzz.*

Why did I have to waste my time like that, digging around in a language I had known since birth and that had caused me, over the years, more than my fair share of problems with teachers ("You're saying it wrong, you're writing it wrong, that's Neapolitan, you don't know how to speak Italian, you make too many spelling mistakes")? Only a few weeks earlier I'd been wondering how to immortalize—because that's the function of literature, Mr. Benagosti had said once after revealing to me that he, too, was a poet—the gracious figure of the girl from Milan by having her speak in writing exactly how she had spoken to me at the fountain. I had wanted to use phonetic writing to reproduce her delightful language as well as I could. But now everything had been downgraded, now I had to go and bother old men and women and ask them for the name of, let's say, the kind of basket they were weaving and when they replied *cuófeno,* I'd have to use my new signs and symbols to write down *cuːofənə.* How idiotic, what a total waste of energy. Was I really renouncing the pleasure of seeing Nina to complete this childish task of filling out index cards?

I was in a terrible mood when I caught sight of my grand-mother. As usual, she was standing at the stove, a withered Vesta next to her sacred fire. After our most recent conver-sation, she had retreated into her role of attentively tending to my each and every need, whether it was providing me with clean socks or a glass of water, her determination com-pounded by the fact that I had shut myself in to study and therefore she could be my servant around the clock and I her distracted lord. I interrupted her musings with a star-tling announcement: Nonna! Good news! The university needs you.

## 23.

Initially, she thought I was joking and mumbled sure, of course, while continuing to tend to something in a sizzling pan. But as soon as I could, I yanked her away from the stove, showed her the books and the index cards I had to fill out, and explained: if you don't help me, I can't take the exam.

It took a while, but when she understood that I was se-rious, all color drained out of her ruddy face, she became flustered, her lower lip trembled, and tears sprang to her eyes, just like when my father humiliated her. Usually, she was willing to do anything for me, but this must have seemed enormous, how could I possibly need her Neapolitan words for my exam. She stammered short, confused phrases, suspicious that someone was pulling a prank on me, or even worse. She giggled nervously and blurted out that the professors might end up using the cards against me, proof that, with a grandmother like her,

I didn't deserve a university degree. She even went as far as comparing me to those aspiring carabinieri who weren't allowed to become officers if their forefathers didn't have clean records. She got so worked up that I felt pain for her.

I tried to calm her down by asking her lots of questions. I wanted to understand what she thought of the university so that I could say no, it's not like that. What slowly emerged was that she imagined it to be the exact opposite of the pit of the dead she had described to me when I was young, which she no longer believed existed.

It wasn't exactly paradise, because she didn't believe in that anymore either, but based on how she gesticulated and the direction her eyes went while she was speaking, for her academia was somewhere high up in the sky, almost in heaven. It was pointless trying to explain that all she had to do to get there was walk straight down the Rettifilo, the entrance was on the right coming out of the station, that she had walked by it countless times. She continued to glance upward and gesture toward the ceiling, the university was up there, and you got there by climbing a kind of staircase that had sifters for steps, because only the purest grains actually made it through. Although she, as a child, had been chucked out almost immediately, even though she knew how to multiply and divide, I, thank goodness, was of a higher quality grain and therefore had every right and privilege to enter that place filled with elegant people, that heavenly white space where no one had to work, everyone spoke in Italian, there was no shouting obscenities like *vafancúlachitèmmuórt* from morning 'til night; people studied, they spent time thinking, and they communicated their ideas with joy and kindness to others whose only concern was providing for their families, people who didn't have time to think.

While it was nice to go back to being a child, it became clear to me as never before that our roles had definitively been reversed. I was now the old one. I was taking advantage of her gullibility as if she were a child. I wanted her to play a game—something like shucking fresh peas or fagioli—that was actually work. I would corner her in the kitchen when everybody else was out of the house and get her to tell me the names of kitchen tools, foods, the ingredients of a certain dish, anything from her world of grandmother-servant, since she—a hard worker, widow since the age of twenty-four, left alone to provide for a two-year-old daughter and a baby in her belly—knew more Neapolitan words than anyone else. I'd write down all those words in the phonetic alphabet and in a matter of hours, with no trouble at all, I'd have my five hundred index cards. As for other interviewees, I'd simply invent them.

### 24.

We talked and she calmed down. I told her that university was not the clean and heavenly place she thought, but that it was dusty, dark, and even musty. However, people studied hard, and my glottology professor was keenly interested in people like her who knew Neapolitan well. I explained to her that professors admired anyone who knew something well, so she didn't have to worry, she'd not only make me look good, but great. Of course, I wouldn't need her for all my exams, definitely not for Italian or for Greek grammar, not even for Latin, but for glottology, yes, for those index cards. Actually, without her help, I would've had to waste tons of time talking to all sorts of people, so I was lucky to have a grandmother like her. Etcetera.

Slowly I managed to convince her, and she started walking around the kitchen, all hunched over, examining things, opening drawers, touching objects she happened upon as if to gather inspiration. She picked up one object, a slotted spoon, smiled with embarrassment, and forced herself to utter the first word of our project. She pronounced the word cautiously, in an unnatural way, as if—seeing that I was the one who needed the word— her usual pronunciation was not good enough, that she needed to refine it somehow. *Pirciatèlla*, she said, dividing up the syllables in her own way: pi-rcia-te-lla. She said it two or three times, slowing down on the -cià and even further on the -lla.

I had the impression she was trying to primp up the word, so that when I went to write it down on that very important index card, it would be worthy of the august circles of the university. Then, forcing herself to speak in Italian, she addressed me as if addressing the professors, or Glottology itself: it's like a *votapésce*—vo-ta-pé-sce—that lets the oil drip through when you fry foods, or like how a *scolapasta*—sco-la-pa-sta—has holes so the water can run out, or like the *pirciatèlla* of a coffee machine, when the dark water comes out and all of a sudden it's *ccafè*— cca-fè—or like *pirciatélli*—pir-rcia-tie-lli—you know, the pasta with the holes in them, *pirciàto*, from *pircià*, the way things filter down through holes, did you get that?

I did, I got it, I wrote it all down in a hurry in phonetics, in pencil: *pirciatèllə, votapescə, uogliə, skolapastə, cafè, pirciatiéllə, percià, perciàtə.* Other words immediately followed suit, a chain of sounds, ever bolder. I was happy but at the same time concerned. My grandmother, it seemed, was standing straighter. It was as if, deep inside her, there was a mass of metallic sounds and that now all that metal was heating up, sentence after sentence, changing the look in her eyes, the expressions on her face, even her bone structure. This struck me as positive and yet I was disturbed by the efforts she was making to sound more dignified. I had told her to speak normally back when she was on *pirciatella*, but to her, in that particular moment, what was normal seemed degrading, and so she resisted. She stubbornly articulated every syllable, even— and this is what annoyed me most—the final ones: *rattacàsa, caccavèlla, tièlla, tiàna, buttéglia, maciniéllo*. This is a *maciniéllo*, she said, and I felt awkward, almost queasy, and at first, I didn't understand why.

Soon enough, my own discomfort revealed what was wrong. I had always hated the way, in dialect, final vowel sounds got dropped and faded into an indistinct sound. Like the way my father yelled at my mother—*addò cazzǝ sí ghiutǝ accussí 'mpennacchiatǝ?*—his jealous words trying to strike her with those -z and -t sounds, but without their endings, without that final syllable, the words just flailed around; teeth that wanted to tear into her flesh instead champed ferociously on air. It reminded me of neighbors arguing, people brawling, or the underhand trafficking that took place across the city that unconsciously led me to associate dialect with rowdiness and disorder. I could never stand how, ever since elementary school, my own habit of using dialect was so strong that it dissolved the endings even of words in proper Italian. To make a good impression on Mr. Benagosti, for the word chalk I immediately forced myself to say *"gesso"* instead of *"gessə."* But, first off, Mr. Benagosti was not that different; even he dropped the final syllables. Secondly, as a young kid, even more than when I was older, I was so susceptible to anxiety that when I was tense, *"quando"* became *"quandə,"* *"allora"* became *"allorə"*; the pronunciation I acquired in my early years had injected me with corrosive poison.

In short, my grandmother's attempt to rise above it was something I knew well; it had shamed me when I was young and still did. Neapolitan, which I had heard and spoken since birth, continued to ambush my Italian, which I had learned mostly from reading. Getting rid of my native language and appropriating the language of books was, still then, a battle, as if I had ordered myself—when exactly, I can't say—to stake a claim on higher ground, a place where I would feel safe. Seeing that same struggle at work in my grandmother, who suddenly seemed as though she could gain access to academia through the transcription of her voice, belittled her and made me seem small. So, at a certain point in our conversation, I said to her even more firmly, as if she was ruining the research and the possible outcome of the exam: you don't need to say it clearly, Nonna, you don't need to Italianize the words. Just speak the way you always do.

She frowned, her eyes welled with tears, and so I quickly praised her, she was doing great, she just had to be who she was, in other words remain within the domain of a grandmother with little schooling. Eventually, she calmed back down, and tried to undo the pretty bow she had tied around her tongue—*'nzèrtə, trébbetə, truóghələ, péttolə, arapabuàttə.* Like that? Did I do good? she asked. Excellent, I replied, and the more I praised her, the more

she continued, the more pleasure she seemed to take in
it—*appésə, appesesacíccia, munígla, cernatúra, scafarèa*—
the more I felt that the awkwardness we initially shared—
the two of us equally uncomfortable with both dialect and
Italian—was transforming into a kind of separation that
was just as awkward, as if she had started running in one
direction—to return to a place of humble dialect—while I
ran in the opposite—to end it all and leap into a place of
noble Italian. To the extent that, if we each left our distant
and separate extremes and met only on the index cards
that were piling up on the table, we probably would've discovered that everything I had written down was as untrue
for her as it was for me.

25.

We spent not just one or two mornings on the research,
but an endless amount of time, measurable only in combinations of sounds and signs, as if the hours were made up of
*buccàla, scummarèlla, chiastulélla, cummuóglia, misuriélla*.
The effects of this task on my grandmother, who spoke,
and on me, who wrote, were starkly different. She, who
started out deeply concerned for my exam, grew more
and more overwhelmed by herself. She ended up inside
the noise in her head, her cheeks and forehead were red
and splotchy, her bell-pepper nose glistened with sweat,
her gaze had been rejuvenated, her eyes were so lively
they seemed to be inhabited by countless other eyes.
She started giving herself airs as never before. When my
brothers came home from school and my father from
work, they peeked in the kitchen to see what was going

on, wondering why there were no smells of food cooking, why the table hadn't been set for lunch, and she'd gleefully reply, we're doing something important for the university, and only then would she make her way over to the stove and say, fine, let's cook a little something. She surprised us all by neglecting to sweep, dust, pick up our dirty clothes, wash them, hang them out to dry, iron them. She even instructed my mother to take care of the cooking and the table for a while, as she was too busy. It was as if the university, by making her the foundation for my studies, had suddenly given her value and granted her freedom from her role as our servant, or anyone's servant for that matter. Even with my father, her sworn enemy, she became less of a subaltern.

"Mother-in-law, what's going on? Are you on strike?"

"Yes."

"And when are you going to start working again?"

"No idea."

This was the only time she even stopped doting on me. The fact that I was the one who hung onto her every word, that she didn't have to run after me with her love, made her overly bold, even impudent (*stattezittonumumènt, ecchecàzz, fammepenzà*), and then she'd come crashing down like a rainstorm, indifferent to whether someone below had an umbrella or not. She was like a pot boiling over, feeling ever more entitled to *sollevare 'o cummuóglia*—to raise the lid—independently of my academic needs, finding immense pleasure in *scummigliarsi*—write it down, Mimí, *scummiglià*, not *cummiglià*, what a beautiful word, you spend your whole life *cummigliàta*, stifled, putting the lid on everything, hidden in fear, and then all of a sudden you *scummuóglia*. To explain better, she mimed someone throwing off their bedding, their clothes, even their silence, and that grand liberatory gesture seemed to bring her joy.

I tried to keep up with her but soon I had more than enough words for the exam. The more cards I filled out, the more it seemed like the entire alphabet and all of phonetic writing were losing ground, unable to keep up with her Neapolitan. Nothing—I thought—will ever be able to stop this merry-go-round, nothing will ever be able to control this uncontrollable material. The more unrestrained she grew, the more inclined I was to wrap it up: basta, why keep collecting words, writing is just another kind of lid being slapped down on this poor old woman, that's enough. And yet, mesmerized, I let her reveal herself, raise her own lid, *scummigliarsi*. Her tone grew richer, the volume of her voice increased, her ardor grew such that in her eyes I saw other eyes, her gestures were those of other people, her mouth was composed of other mouths, in her words were endless words belonging to other people, her voice so dysregulated that no tool could ever record it, much less the act of writing. Oh, how much time I was wasting. Thanks to my studies, with practice, I could, at the very least, hope to bring structure and shape to the echoes of the voice of the girl from Milan; they were like a gift. But the teeming sounds uttered by my grandmother were impossible to get down on a clean sheet of paper: literature retreated, the alphabet backed down, even phonetic writing came up short. At one point, it seemed like it wasn't just her talking, but her mother, her grandmother, her great-grandmother, speaking words that were pre-Babelic, antediluvian, words about the earth, plants, bodily humors, blood, work, an entire dictionary of the struggles she had survived, another dictionary of critical illnesses that struck both children and adults. *L'artéteca*—she/they said—was an intolerable disquietude that you can't calm; *riscenziéla* was that sensation of falling, fainting, eyes rolling back into your head; and then there was loving and kissing, *il bacio, 'o vase, ah vasarsi*, Mimí, there's nothing better on this earth than kissing, hugging, squeezing each other tight, and if you don't understand kissing, well what good is all this studying?

She spent an endless amount of time talking about that subject. She told me about the first kiss her husband ever gave her, back when he was a young and terribly handsome twenty-year-old, and she already twenty-two but had never been kissed: a kiss that was so intense that he had stayed right there in her mouth, to this day his mouth was in her mouth, his voice was her voice, they spoke together when she spoke, the words that I heard came from the depths of time, his breath and hers, his voice and hers.

## 26.

We ended with the kiss. My grandmother fished around for more words, couldn't find any, and declared that she had said everything there was to say. While retreating with my index cards into the small room where I studied with the door closed, I heard her singing with surprising vigor, carefully pronouncing the endings: *vento, vento, portami via con te*. Then she stopped and I don't recall ever hearing her sing again.

I often thought back to her nostalgia for kisses. Maybe I kissed Nina hurriedly. Her eyes and her mouth bewitched me, but I was always overcome with desire for other parts of her body. If my grandmother still remembers her husband's kisses after forty years, I told myself, maybe kisses are important to Nina, too, maybe she wants to be kissed more often and with greater intensity. I had no time to remedy the situation, though; as exam day was fast approaching, I talked to her rarely and saw her even less. At that point in time, I was concerned more with the oral cavity not as it pertained to lovers but for the sake of glottology. I had to memorize charts and be able to distinguish all different kinds of consonants: bilabial, labiodental, dental, dento-alveolar, retroflexed, palato-alveolar, alveolar-palatal, palatal, velar, uvular, pharyngeal, laryngeal. And while this lexicon gradually and increasingly erased Nina's mouth, I found that it increasingly had me thinking about the mouth of the girl from Milan, what hers would've been like if she'd been able to grow up and utter occlusive, nasal, vibrant, fricative, semi-vocals, and vocals in the same elegant tone that she used when she spoke to me at the fountain. Who can say what she would've gone on to study, in addition to dance, of course, maybe modern literature and languages, or maybe ancient languages, like me. We could've discussed phonetic writing together, we could've talked about Boehmer, Ascoli, Battisti, Merlo, Jaberg and Jud, and Forchhammer. And in the meantime, who knows, I might've enjoyed kissing her (or rather, ˈkɪsɪŋ hɜr) and whispering sweet nothings into her mouth while she whispered them into mine, ad infinitum.

Now and then I stepped out of my room in a daze and tried to call Nina. When I managed to find her at home, our conversations usually went like this:

"How's it going with algebra?"

"Fine. How about you with glottology?"

"Studying hard."

"Are you done with your grandmother?"

"Yes."

"Want me to come over?"

"Better not, I'm behind on the toponyms of Abruzzo and Molise."

"Do you still love me?"

"Yes, what about you?"

"Yes."

Then one day she said, "I talked to your friend. He's having a hard time with math."

"Ah."

"I offered to tutor him."

"What about your algebra exam?"

"You do a lot of tutoring and still study. So can I."

"But I get paid."

"Actually, he wants to pay me."

"When will you start?"

"Tomorrow."

"Will he come over to your house?"

"No, it's too noisy here. I'll go to the cemetery."

"You're going to give him lessons in the chapel? Next to the burial niche where he keeps his bread and salami?"

"Yeah. I'll make a little money, and it'll also be fun."

It upset me but I didn't say anything. She seemed irritable and I didn't want to argue. My imagined cemetery annoyed, but a real one was fun. For the first time, I noticed the Neapolitan cadence in her Italian. Like me, she sometimes Italianized her dialect (for example, when she thought I was playfully teasing her, she'd ask, "*Mi stai sfruculiando?*"). Like me, she often used Neapolitan syntactical structures in Italian (for example, she'd say "*Quello è lui che mi prende in giro*"). Like me, she had a hard time holding onto the vowel endings of words (for example, on the phone she always said "*Prontə*" instead of "*Pronto*"). I went back to my books thinking that if I wanted to write with absolute truth about our relationship, and therefore also about our conversations, the resulting text would be twisted, corroded, readable by few, and impossible to translate; the opposite of what was required to fulfill Mr. Benagosti's prophecy, which saw my works traveling from city to city, country to country, language to language, appreciated by millions of readers.

## 27.

A few days before the glottology exam—after which I'd immediately have to start studying for papyrology— my thoughts, which were already something of a mess, got even messier. I was in my little room, trying to memorize the toponyms of Abruzzo and Molise by repeating them out loud, when the door opened, and my grandmother came in. She looked smaller than usual, was more hunched over than usual, and her usual ruddy color had disappeared from her face. She apologized for disturbing me but there was no one home she could talk to. Her knees were shaking, she felt like vomiting, everything had suddenly gone black.

I sat her down and got her a glass of water, and slowly the color returned to her face. Sluggishly, as if her tongue didn't want to obey, she told me that the feeling had come over her right when she realized that it was almost November 2, the day of the dead, and therefore her husband's feast day. It's been so long, she'd thought to herself, and then she felt a shudder run through her.

"Do you feel any better now?"

"Yes."

But she didn't get up, she didn't go back to the kitchen, she said she was scared that she'd feel sick and die before being able to go to her husband's burial niche and celebrate him.

"That's not going to happen," I said firmly to reassure her.

"But what if it does?"

"Then I'll go and tell Nonno that you have a good excuse."

She burst out laughing and leaned over to give me a kiss of gratitude, but I moved out of the way. Her presence was making it hard for me to get any studying done. She, who had never wanted anything from me, now clearly did. She beat around the bush for a while and then finally asked if, after my exam, I'd accompany her to the cemetery. She had saved up to buy a *pezzotto* with four votive lights. I didn't say yes.

"After glottology, I have to study for another exam."

"Oh."

"Why do you want someone to go with you?"

"I might fall."

"But you always go on your own."

"I'm scared I won't make it."

"Why?"

"This morning old age arrived."

I looked at her sitting limply in my chair in that little room and recalled not only the voices of the many dead people who inhabited her, but also what a beautiful young woman she had been and how that young woman was probably lurking somewhere inside her body, protecting the kisses she had both given and received. Again, I felt pain for her.

"Fine," I said, "you helped me out, I can do the same for you."

"Thank you."

But then I was the one who kept her from going back to her tasks. I couldn't get the image of that young widow out of my head and so I asked, "After Nonno died, didn't anyone else ask you to marry them?"

Although she still looked unwell, the topic was interesting, and she perked up.

"Of course, I had tons of suitors."

This comment led to a detailed conversation which I quickly wrote down and relate here, without trying to capture her Neapolitan—I'm tired of my futile attempt to imitate her.

"Why didn't you get remarried?"

"Because I never liked anyone as much as I liked my husband."

"But he died."

"Just because someone dies, doesn't mean you stop liking them."

"But after a while, you forget about them."

"*Non mi va di scordare*, I don't want to forget."

"Why?"

"Well, if your *chord* breaks you can't play the mandolin anymore."

"Nonna, the word *scordare* has the word for heart in it, *cor*—not chord."

"Even better: if you forget, your heart breaks. And if

your heart breaks, you die. But I'm not dead, I haven't forgotten my husband, and therefore, he's alive."

I thought about it for a moment. "I don't want to forget
either."

"Who?"

She delicately asked me if I had been in love with someone else before Nina, someone I couldn't get out of my
head. I told her it wasn't a matter of love, but of memories that had never entirely disappeared, and I didn't know
why. She started muttering that if I was thinking about
somebody else, that meant I didn't love Nina, the poor girl,
she was so pretty. That's when I realized something that I
had never fully expressed, not even to myself. I told her
that Nina had just come along, and that what comes along
in life is not the same as what you choose. I definitely had
strong feelings for her, but there were other things besides
her that filled my head and that moved me. I listed them for
her: reading, writing, and death. My desire to live, Nonna,
is so violent that I always feel like my life is in danger, which
makes me want to hold onto it even tighter, so it can't get
away from me and end; I've had this feeling ever since that
girl died, the girl who used to play on the third floor balcony of the light blue building across the street. At that
point, I needed to be completely sure she understood who
I meant.

"Do you remember the girl from Milan?" I asked.

"What girl from Milan?"

"The one who used to play on the balcony of the building across the street from ours, and then drowned. How
can you not remember?"

Puzzled, my grandmother looked at me. "She wasn't
from Milan, and she didn't drown."

"Yes, she was."

She shook her head. "She was from Naples, just like you and me, and she died with her grandfather, Professor Paucillo. They were run over by a car while they were coming back from the beach by bicycle."

### 28.

These days I'm so used to such small shocks that when they happen, I am no longer able to feel surprise. My life has become predictable to the point that when I wake up in the morning, I almost find myself hoping that something bad will happen, something that'll make me say: well now, I never expected that to happen. I'm so well trained not to be amazed by anything anymore—I've heard and seen and read and imagined and lived through far too much—that I wouldn't even be shocked if someone said: seeing how so many older people have died in truly atrocious ways of late, from this day forward, as decreed by the heavenly father, the elderly will no longer die. If only to be able to recall exactly what happened in the past, I wish that I could unscrew my head, clean it out, and screw it back on again, just so that I could exclaim, as incredulously as I did sixty years ago: what? The girl from Milan was really from Naples?

"You know who I'm talking about, right?" I added quietly.

"Yes."

"If you do, you can't possibly be telling the truth."

"I never lie."

"But you are now. That girl spoke the most beautiful Italian I've ever heard."

"No surprise there. She was the daughter and grand-daughter of professors, after all. Even her grandmother was a teacher. I remember I used to think she was the kind of woman who'd lord it over me, but actually she was very kind and decent. Whenever I bumped into her at the butcher's, she was always the first to say hello. Two or three times I even saw her at the cemetery. We talked a little, bought our *pezzotti*, and bickered with the people who sold the lights, because they're all crooks, you know, they take your money and then the lights don't work, or they work for a little bit and then go out."

My grandmother knew absolutely everything about Professoressa Paucillo, the girl's paternal grandmother. She had lovely hair and was always so elegant. She used to visit her husband and granddaughter's graves, oh, the tragedies that strike families are unimaginable. She went to the cemetery every holy day to say hello, that's what she used to say: I came to say hello. What a fine person she was. My grandmother was sorry she stopped bumping into her. Maybe Professoressa Paucillo had gotten tired of saying hello to her husband and granddaughter, or maybe death had taken her, too. I kept hoping that she'd say something to contradict herself, I asked questions, tried to figure out if maybe the girl's mother, or relatives, or forefathers were from Milan. No, no, no. My grandmother assured me that all of them, each and every one, were Neapolitan, and even added: that's why I'm glad you're studying, and that you'll become a professor, too. I decided to ask.

"What was the girl's name?"

"Manuela Paucillo."

"Why didn't you ever tell me about her?"

"What was I supposed to say?"

"Everything."

"You were young and too sad."

"You should've told me everything."

"You always had a fever, you used to cry in your sleep, you have no idea how worried I was. Children should never learn about death."

"That's not true."

"Yes, it is. Once you learn about death, you stop growing."

## 29.

In the final days before the exam, I studied little. I got distracted easily and wrote page after page about the girl no longer from Milan. I tried to recover from the letdown, or at least understand the reasons behind it. I came to terms with the fact that, just like all the other kids in the piazza, including Lello with his own version of Italian, I had made a mistake: that ethereal figure who had spoken to me at the gurgling fountain in a commingling of bookish language and extremely clear Neapolitan had seemed completely foreign to Naples. Actually, maybe—I said to myself to settle my nerves—those beloved undertones in her voice, which I guarded so jealously in my memory and wished I could capture with phonetic writing, were nothing other than the residue of my own dialect spoken in the gracious way she had learned to speak it in her family since birth.

The day before the exam, I tried to call Nina, to both share my discovery with her and ask her to come to the glottology exam and wait with me until it was my turn to sit before the professor. But she wasn't home, so I tried

Lello. He answered. I started by asking him to put aside a *pezzotto* with room for eight electric votives for November 2 for my grandmother as she was eager to give her husband the gift of abundant light. Lello was as helpful as usual, but his voice sounded different, still cordial and friendly, but impatient, as if he was in a hurry to end the conversation. But I had more to tell him.

"Have you come up with anything more about the girl from Milan?" I asked.

"To tell the truth, no," he said.

"We always used to call her that because we didn't know her name."

"Yeah, could be."

"Her name was Manuela Paucillo—what an ugly name, she was better off without it."

"Ah."

"And she actually wasn't from Milan."

"Ah."

"She was Neapolitan."

"That's why I couldn't remember her, you confused me."

"You were the one who confused me! You must've invented that she was from Milan."

"No, that's impossible. I can't invent anything."

I laughed in agreement and went on. "But what you can do is have a look in your registers or files at the cemetery and tell me where her grave is. I'd like to order a *pezzotto* with eight candles for her, too."

"Your wish is my command. How long do you want the lights to stay lit for? One day? Two? Three?"

"Two days is fine. One more thing, and then I'll let you go. I called Nina and she's not home. Do you know where she is?"

Silence.

"She's here," he said.

"What's she doing there?"

"She's helping me with math."

"Oh."

"Do you want to talk to her?"

"Sure, put her on."

I heard Nina laugh in the background. When she answered the phone, I knew right away that the era of gentleness between us had come to its definitive end.

"What are you doing there," I asked.

"Having a coffee."

"Just the two of you?"

"Me, him, and his mother. Three coffees. If you want to join us, we'll wait for you. That'll make four coffees."

"I can't. I have my exam tomorrow."

"Fine, so I'll go ahead and have my coffee now, then, without you."

"The session starts at eleven. I'm nervous. Will you come with me?"

Silence.

"Yes."

## 30.

My name was called, and Nina still hadn't arrived. I sat down in front of the examiners, my heart beating fast. The professor with the soft voice asked me if I could name a toponym in Abruzzo—How many b's are there in Abbruzzo? Spelling mistakes are resurfacing in my old age; will death be the collapse of what little English, French, and Italian I know? Will I forget how to spell? Will I shatter to pieces inside my grandmother's dialect? Will I get upset and melt like some rhetorical figure?—a toponym composed of a noun and an adjective. I answered quickly: Campotosto. Immediately after, he asked me about Hellwag's famous triangle of vowels and I handled that pretty well, with only some hesitation here and there. But when he started asking me questions about Forchhamer's lalemics, I unfortunately drew a blank, and still to this day I don't know what they are. To make up for it, I spoke confidently and at length about the index cards, phonetic writing, and my grand-mother, who was once a glove maker but now a housewife and who spoke an uncontaminated dialect. I lied about the condition of her teeth and said that despite being sixty-five she still had almost all of them, thank goodness. It was bril-liant. My examiner spoke enthusiastically about the role of grandmothers in society, praised me for valuing mine, told me to thank her warmly for her help, and, when it was all done, gave me a final grade of twenty-seven out of thirty, which seemed very high and an auspicious beginning to my academic career. I was happy with how well I had hidden my ignorance.

I walked out of the lecture room bowled over by my suc-cess, looking around for Nina in the cold and bleak Cortile del Salvatore. I saw her immediately, but she wasn't alone, she was with Lello. They stood about a meter apart as if they didn't know each other, but all it took was one glance to understand that they stood together in a ring of fire, like the grand finale of an equestrian number at the circus. I walked over to them in a hurry.

"How did it go?" Lello asked.

"Twenty-seven."

"Bravo."

"I would've bet on it," Nina said.

I was so happy that I couldn't free up—not with the two of them standing there like that, so clearly eager to brush up against each other, even if it meant just touching arms—the sense of despair that was lurking inside me. I pointed at them, waggling my finger first at one and then at the other ironically.

"Are you two dating?"

Lello looked at me remorsefully. "Not yet. We wanted to tell you first."

"He wanted to," Nina clarified. "I didn't. It's the kind of thing that if it happens, it happens."

"And it happened."

"Yes."

"Why?"

Lello interrupted us with some embarrassment. "There's no reason."

I turned to him, as seriously as I possibly could. "So, what are we going to do about it?"

"What do you mean?"

"I mean, do we resolve it with a duel?"

Lello laughed, I laughed, Nina got annoyed.

"Why do you always have to joke around, even when we're talking about serious stuff?" she asked.

"I'm not joking. If we duel, he dies, I let off steam, and that way I no longer feel the need to kill you."

"You know what your problem is? You never grew up."

"And according to you, what do I need to do to grow up?"

"I don't know."

Even though I continued to act like I was in a good

mood, Lello surely noticed how upset I was, and he helped me out by changing the subject.

"I brought you the receipt for the *pezzotti*. I gave you a discount. I only charged you eighty lire for each light bulb."

I looked at the total and paid him.

"Thanks," I said.

"Thank you," he replied. "For everything: I never forgot your grandfather's sword or the pit of the dead. You told such good stories. Also, I found out where the girl's burial niche is located. Are you going to write a scary story about her?"

I shook my head, aware that my good cheer was fading fast. "You really don't remember her?"

"Honestly, no."

Nina interrupted us. Now she spoke in a pained voice that seemed almost sincere. "See? You make it so easy to stop caring for you."

She was right. Maybe to let someone love me the way Lello let himself be loved, I'd have to quit inventing stories about everything, the same way I'd quit dueling with my grandfather's sword. But I quickly realized that if I gave up on writing, just as I had stopped believing I was capable of a fair number of other things, not only would I be proving Mr. Benagosti wrong, but I'd also be forced to accept that there was nothing exceptional about me at all.

I turned to her and said, "This *strunz* doesn't know a damn thing about the girl from Milan because I haven't written the story yet. But if I do, you can be sure he'll remember her, and Manuela Paucillo, despite her first and last name, will become immortal."

I did an about-face, ran to the first payphone, and called my grandmother to tell her about the exam.

"Pronta," she shouted anxiously.

I shouted back my reply. "We did good, Nonna! We got a twenty-seven, a really good grade."

## 31.

I kept my promise and accompanied my grandmother to the cemetery to celebrate her husband on the day of the dead. Even though it was only ten o'clock in the morning, it was dark out, a salty wind blew hard, and damp black rain clouds hung heavily over the city. Except for when I was small, when she swore she took me around Naples for fresh air and sunshine, either carrying me or walking hand in hand, we had never gone out together. This was the only time.

It was anything but easy. The city streets were jammed with traffic, crowded buses inched forward slowly, the road to the cemetery was one long procession of families on their way to say hello to their loved ones. My grandmother seemed awfully fragile, she walked slowly and leaned on my arm, wearing her one black dress and holding her purse tightly to her chest out of fear of thieves. Eventually, we arrived. When we reached my grandfather's burial niche, she let go of my arm slowly and stood sedately in front of the marble plaque with its three brownish photographs and three names: that of her husband and his mother and father. The photo of her husband, the man who had fallen to his death, showed him looking young and strong. If he could've seen my grandmother, he probably would've said: who the hell is this? The wet marble sparkled from all the votive lights on the *pezzotto* that Lello had applied to a strip of metal that he had installed in the groove between the burial niche cover and the ledge.

"It's so beautiful with all this light," my grandmother said, sighing with satisfaction under the dome of her umbrella.

"I went over the top," I said, "I told him to put up eight lights."

"Better to live large than be stingy."

"Are you going to pray now?"

"No."

"Then what're you going to do?"

"I'm going to talk to him a little bit in my head."

I nodded and asked her if I could leave her on her own for ten minutes without running the risk that she'd go wandering off and that I'd lose her. Concerned, she asked me what I had to do that was so urgent that it couldn't wait, and I lied and told her I had seen a friend and wanted to say hello. She begrudgingly gave me permission but as soon as I got to the end of the path, she shouted: don't run, be careful, don't hurt yourself.

I found the custodian and showed him the paper that Lello had given me with the location of the girl's grave. He told me how to get there: go right, then left, then up some stairs, then down some stairs, and off I went under the rain and dark sky to the Paucillo family crypt, where the gate sat open even though not a soul—living, at any rate—was around. It was as if it had been abandoned, inside I found rotting leaves brought in on the wind, scorpions, shrews, hairy spiders. The only thing that shone brightly was the *pezzotto* with eight votives that Lello had set up in front of the plaque that read: EMANUELA PAUCILLO, 1944-1952.

I put on a doleful face and listened to the sound of the rain and to the scurrying mice for a while. But then I couldn't resist, I took out a piece of paper and pen and wrote: do you mind if, for the rest of my life, I continue to call you the girl from Milan? Then I folded up the piece of paper and slipped it into one of the two cross-shaped fissures in the marble. I was pulling my hand away when the eight votive lights suddenly went out, and the crypt sank into darkness.

I got scared and thought that maybe Emanuela Paucillo wanted to reclaim her true identity, so I rushed back to my grandmother in the drizzling rain. She was raging mad, as were all the other relatives near her who were visiting their dead. Everybody was screaming and yelling: this always happens, every single day of the dead. They paid all that money for lights—to those thieves, tricksters, swindlers, sonsofbitches—that worked at first, then flickered, then came on again, then *stutavano* forever.

"Well, if that's the case," I said eagerly, "we have to go and complain."

"Yes," my grandmother agreed.

Five or six of us started down the path, with my grandmother and I out in front. Along the way, we encountered other clusters of unhappy relatives who had also spent good money to bring their loved ones as much light as possible, and now, despite having paid, down there—they said, pointing to the earth, now muddy with rain—it was darker than ever.

We reached the main mausoleum and crowded around its entrance. It was pitch black inside, too, and people there were even more irate. We joined forces with other mourners on the ground floor, while families on the floors above, where entire walls of niches had gone dark, leaned out over the railings and shouted down insults: harsh words and wild phrases, insults having to do with orifices that had been violated or soon would be, together with the sound of people slapping themselves weakly in preparation to slap others much harder—the debt collectors, the electricians, and the debt collector-electricians—in front of whom they'd soon be waving their receipts.

My grandmother felt linguistically at ease, I less so; I was educated and would've preferred protesting in Italian. Moreover, it was not some dodgy racketeering gang facing the crowd, but Lello—with his nice round face, like a blond Norwegian sailor—and—standing next to him, maybe just visiting or maybe recently hired—Nina. At first, I felt a little worried for them, but then I relaxed. I looked at them and saw how perfectly matched, invincible, and well-equipped they were to deal with the furies of the world. They'd sort everything out capably and maturely, first by striking awe into the crowd and then by promising, in their university-student Italian with its light Neapolitan inflection, the immediate restoration of light. The only thing they were feeling in that particular moment was the fullness of life. They were so happy about being together that they would've been content in even the direst situations: in a police station, among the sick and wounded in an emergency room, at war, and, of course, standing in front of a crowd of angry mourners. Even when I looked at them, those two glowing vendors of light, I only saw the very faintest fringe of death.

## 32.

I made the effort and erased even that, the way a cloud goes dark at the edges when the sun tries to break through. I stayed their friend, asked about their exams, was happy for them when they passed without a care for any difficulties or struggles they might have faced. Naturally the three of us never went out again, but I did bump into them on various occasions: at parties, a birthday, a friend's wedding. We even took an English class together.

My knowledge of English has never been particularly dazzling, especially spoken. I was like someone who wanted to sing but was tone deaf. When the teacher forced us to engage in conversation, no one understood me, not even the teacher. But Nina and Lello were truly gifted. For example, I remember how, with perfect pronunciation, they said: *This Side of Paradise* was Fitzgerald's first book, a sensational story that shocked the nation and skyrocketed the author to fame. When I listened to them say things like that, I felt happy for them, and could finally see their futures buoyant, untouched by grief. They were beautiful and blessed. I bumped into them not too long ago, and even though they're old now, with three children already around the age of fifty, they're still stunning, just like they were when they were young. It's as if the notion that, one day, they'll have to lift the cover and descend into the pit of the dead doesn't even go through their heads. In fact, they probably never will.

As for me, my story is a swift one. I decided not to take the papyrology exam because it gave me panic attacks, I was fed up with Vesuvius, its eruption, and how chance had saved texts by Philodemus but not those of others.

I even regretted leaving that piece of paper in Emanuela Paucillo's burial niche. I imagined the scholar who, in a couple thousand years, would find it, read it, and try to decipher what it meant. I planned on going back to the cemetery at night, removing the marble slab, retrieving the piece of paper, and destroying all embarrassing traces that could potentially survive me. When I thought back to the crypt, I brushed it aside, and instead tried to imagine Emanuela at university, like her ancestors: pretty, erudite, capable of speaking French, English, and German, well-paired with a well-off man. Look at her move through life, shining even brighter than Nina, traveling across Naples, capable of confidently shifting from her truly elegant Italian to a dialect narrower than the one my grandmother spoke, the way well-bred families of this terrible and marvelous city have always been able to do.

During that feverish period of re-education, I went back to falling in love. I liked the sound of girls' voices, and even though I was a long way away from receiving my degree (the only exam I took that session was glottology), I started going out with a girl with the goal of getting married young. Encouraged by my future wife, I tried to write short stories but did so halfheartedly, without conviction. I'd read something, let's say, about Caio Giulio Cesare, and I'd jot down a tale about his scribe, who, unable to keep up with his master while he dictated the *Commentaries* to him, gradually transformed into Vercingetorix. Or else I'd be reading *The Brothers Karamazov* and I'd invent a young man who, in order to live his own life, had to pay the taxman the weight of his father's portly body in gold. Or I'd read something about the spread of poverty across the planet and I'd imagine a story about a deeply sensitive but very fat man who allowed himself to be tied to hot metal bars affixed to the ceiling so that he could slowly melt, drip by drip, into containers arranged underneath him by the hungry people of his neighborhood. Or I would read something about kidney transplants and invent a story about a city employee who was so depressed that his eyeballs literally fell out of their sockets, which allowed him to look at things, and himself especially, in a way that he'd never been able to do before.

Since my girlfriend, whom I forced to read those stories, inevitably exclaimed: what infinite despair there is in all your characters, one evening I was forced to point out how, if I scratch away at the surface of even the liveliest letter, I always find a dead one. The following morning, I said to myself: basta, time to forget about being exceptional, of being skyrocketed—oh, how I loved that word—to fame with your debut novel; literature has nothing to do with will-power, time to downgrade, scale back. I was who I was, just another mass of living and decaying matter, enough with the childish delusions. And so, I put one foot in front of the other and enrolled in a course of study that wasn't excessively hard, I obtained a degree without too much struggle, I got a solid job that I did honestly, I took on the role of faithful husband and affectionate father and enjoyed a life of contentment. Once all that had been accomplished, I prepared myself to grow old prematurely, and make an art of it, as if an addiction.

It wouldn't be honest of me if I didn't mention that helping me through that final feverish growth phase was my grandmother, and she did so by falling ill and dying. With her disappearance from this earth, I unequivocally lost the urge to achieve great things, and years later, when I went back to writing, I did so with rational passion, knowing full well that the little life we truly live always remains in the margins, that marks and signs are constitutionally inadequate, fluctuating merely between what you try to say and pure dismay, and thank goodness it is thus. I allowed myself only one small concession, which I permit myself to this day: the pleasure of choosing a word that seems right in one moment and then does not; the pleasure that flows through your body even if you're writing with water on stone on a hot summer day, without ever caring about approval, or truth, or lies, or raising issues or sowing the seeds of hope, or how long something might endure, or memory, or immortality or any of the rest of it.

The problem, if there is one, is that that the pleasure of writing is fragile, it has a hard time making it up the slippery slope of real life. For decades I've been telling myself: now I'm going to write about Lello, Nina, Manuela Paucillo and, most of all, about my grandmother, but I keep putting them aside in favor of things that seem to have more heft. Sure, it's true, Marcel Proust rediscovered his grandmother while looking for lost time in *Sodom and Gomorrah*. But if mine couldn't even stand up to Emanuela Paucillo's grandmother, how on earth would she ever handle Proust's? I'd put her down on the page and only a few lines later I had to put her away in dejection.

What it took for me to try again was the hallucinated certainty of having caught a glimpse of her—hunched over, with her bell pepper nose, extremely short—already carefully written about in a slight book that was just her size. All I have to do—I told myself—is put white spaces between words, now and then start a new paragraph, number the chapters, and it's done. So, I started sketching it out, day after day, right up until this very morning, using the two or three baubles totally lacking in any psychological, historical, and linguistic elegance that she left in my memory as a starting point. Like the time I asked her: Nonna, how does a person die? Or the time she helped me out with the glottology exam, when I had to buy, in addition to a few other textbooks, a slender volume of less than a hundred pages that cost 1100 lire, written by Aniello Gentile, and entitled *Elementi di grafia fonetica*—which I later lost—a book that was essential for learning how to write down the words in Neapolitan uttered by the elderly. To make things easier for me, I had chosen to consult my grandmother, Anna Di Lorenzo, who had always lived at home with us. But since no one actually called her by her real name, it took enormous effort to recall that she was indeed named Anna. To her numerous sisters she was always Nanní, for my mother she was mammà, for my father she was mother-in-law, and for us four grandsons she was Nonnà, with the accent on the final -a. Nonnà! we shouted urgently or demanded with irritation, always expecting her to obey us immediately. Sometimes she tried to run away to spite my father, but my brothers and I always grabbed her before she reached the final flight of stairs. She always seemed ancient to us, she was always shut inside her chores, submissive and mute, so that we were surprised and alarmed when she suddenly rose up and attempted to flee.

Once—I remember—I came home late, I had been out all day, the house was messy, and everybody was upset. My mother was crying, there was water on the kitchen floor, a chair had been knocked over, one of my grandmother's old slippers lay in the hall—she who was always so orderly—the other in the doorway of the room where she slept with my brothers. Something had touched her brain, a neighbor said. First it had made her nose bleed, and then her mouth stayed twisted to one side, and she couldn't speak. She stopped cooking and cleaning and sat crumpled up in a chair next to the kitchen window for weeks. She looked at me with the same affection in her glazed-over eyes, and when I sat around the house doing nothing, she'd try and talk to me, but it was impossible to understand what she was saying.

Months passed, and then one morning she didn't get out of bed. My father yelled that she needed oxygen—a tank—but there was none to be found. He didn't say: go find an oxygen tank or else your grandmother will die. He didn't even pull out his wallet, seeing how we kids didn't have much money and certainly not enough to buy oxygen if we had found it in some pharmacy somewhere. He said it with despair, either to himself or to the ceiling, to the heavens and to the saints, but definitely not to me or my brother. Even so, we ran out, rushed down the stairs, and hurried off toward Piazza Garibaldi and Forcella, less concerned with saving our grandmother, I think, than escaping the unbearable fact that she was dying.

In fact, when we came back without oxygen, she had already died. I often think about how many relatives, both close and distant, and how many friends and acquaintances have died over the decades. I make a careful list, beginning with the girl and my grandmother, and can't help but marvel at how numerous they are, strangely, more even than those who died in the plague this year and last. My grandmother was the first lifeless person I ever saw. Her skin was pale and looked as though it had been draped over her nose and stretched across her cheekbones like a handkerchief. I kissed her forehead and discovered she was the temperature of a flower vase, a sugar bowl, a pen, or the sewing machine on a winter's day. I felt a deep and violent pain in my chest, and immediately regretted that kiss. With her death came the definitive end to the girl from Milan.

## About the Author

Best-selling and critically acclaimed novelist Domenico Starnone is considered by many to be Italy's greatest living author. He was born in 1943 in Naples and currently lives in Rome. He is the author of fifteen works of fiction, including: *Ties*, a *New York Times* Editors Pick and Notable Book of the Year, and a *Sunday Times* and *Kirkus Reviews* Best Book of the Year; *Trick*, a finalist for the 2018 National Book Award and the 2019 PEN Translation Prize; and, *Trust*, "a short, sharp novel that cuts like a scalpel to the core of its characters" (*LA Times*). Starnone's most recent novel to be published in English is the Strega Prize-winning *The House on Via Gemito*, a *Washington Post* and *Kirkus Reviews* Best Book of the Year and *New York Times* Editors Choice. It was long-listed for the 2024 International Booker Prize. Starnone is the recipient of all three of Italy's major literary prizes: The Strega prize, the Napoli prize, and the Campiello prize.